Bob Moats

I0567408

FATAL DEPARTURE

By Bob Moats

Copyright © 2011-2014 by Bob Moats.

Rev. 0416140045

1

Fatal Departure

ISBN - 978-0-9903138-9-2

For information and address:
Magic 1 Productions
P.O. Box 524, Fraser MI 48026-0524
Website: http://murdernovels.com
Cover by Bob Moats

Bob Moats

My thanks to:

To Jan Kimball for editing my story. She checked my first couple books way back in 2009.

To all the Beta readers, especially Al Norris, who hates all of my books but he still reads them, and makes sure he points out all the mistakes he finds.

A special thanks to all the faithful readers of my books, without you this wouldn't be fun anymore, thanks!

Advanced Reviews from the beta readers:

Fatal Departure by Bob Moats is a masterpiece, fraught with suspense and mystery, as well as Moats' usual dab of humor. This is the sequel to Fatal Rejection, which you should read first. In Fatal Departure, a serial killer is leaving body parts around the town, taunting the Sheriff who calls in the FBI for support. This killer has the same modus operandi of successive killings in Seattle two years ago. This is a real page turning murder/mystery that is gripping and riveting. The author and former magician really pulled a rabbit out of his hat with this one. A must read!

RJ Parker - Author of True Crime Files

3

The Author

Bob Moats is the author of 40 novels about a senior citizen sleuth named Jim Richards, starting with the first book of the series, "Classmate Murders". He wrote the short fantasy novella "Crystal Prison of Kyr" and is a published playwright with his three act comedy "Happily Ever After".

To read more about Bob's books, go to
http://bobmoats.com.

Departure: "A euphemistic expression for death"

Chapter 1

She crashed through the brambles, scratching her face, hands and tearing her clothing. The monster was gaining fast, as she stumbled on a rotten tree limb on the ground, catching herself. She ran on into the dark foreboding woods deeper than she had ever gone before, causing her to lose her direction. She didn't care, the creature behind her was gaining, which was worse than being lost. Hearing the thing howling and snarling behind her, made her move faster.

She tried to climb a tall embankment, pulling at limbs and roots, trying to get a foothold in the crumbling dirt. She felt a hand on her ankle pulling her back, she kicked and tried to pull away, but the hand held on. She was afraid to look back, to see the monster's face. She pulled herself up as the hand slipped its grip and she reached the top of the drop-off. She was now in an open field, no hiding places. She kept running forward as she heard the fiend coming over the crest.

The field went on forever as she kept pace ahead of her pursuer. She was losing breath and getting dizzy, she wanted to sit down in the middle of the field. Exhausted now, she sat down and gave up. As she sat, she looked back in tears as the shadowy figure came rushing up and stopped above her holding the huge knife in its hand. She closed her eyes and waited, as her head was pulled back, the knife slit her throat draining the blood and life from her. She tried to scream but couldn't, then it finally escaped her mouth. She screamed loud and long.

"What the hell?" came a voice from her left. She woke to see Dave in bed next to her, sitting up. "Are you all right, babe?"

Sweat was pouring down Sarah's face as she tried to sit up. Dave helped and put his arm around her. "It's alright; you just had a bad dream."

"Oh, God. It was horrible. I was running and running, trying to escape from something. It had no form, just a dark shadow," she cried and turned to her live-in love, Sheriff Dave Chandler and said, "I'm not sure which serial killer it was." She was talking about the serial killers that she fought off three months ago in her former house, south of Brinnon, Washington. The killers were given a ticket to hell and Sarah was safe.

She and Dave had lived in his apartment for about a month after her house was put up for sale. They looked at a small house that her friend and real estate agent, Lois Carter, showed them. It was a cute three bedroom house, with a big fenced in yard that her dog, Van Gogh could run in. She named the dog after the painter, because the dog was missing part of one ear. Sarah's former husband, who was murdered by one of the serial killers, was an artist and he liked Vincent Van Gogh.

"This is the second time you've had these dreams. Maybe you should see someone before they get worse?" Dave asked.

"I'm not seeing a shrink. I don't need a shrink. I'm not crazy."

"I didn't say you are crazy, you're not. But we know the reason you are having these dreams. You should at least give it a try. Maybe it can help you to get past the memory."

"Yeah, well Brinnon doesn't have a shrink."

"Actually, there is a psychiatrist in town. She helps people with the stress of living in a small town." He laughed. "No, really, she's a great shrink, but don't call her that."

"Is she one of the three women you've slept with in your sordid past." She smiled and slapped him on the arm, laying back and pulling him to her. She kissed him and grabbed his ass.

"Hey, I'm not cheap. So are you going to see her?"

"If I say no, will it affect any sex between us?"

"It may, I don't like you screaming in the night."

"You like my screaming when we have sex," she said with a smile.

"Yes, and you sound like a banshee in heat."

"Screw you."

"I hope so." He smiled, kissed her, then they went back to sleep.

7

Fatal Departure

Dave got up around seven and dressed to go to fight crime. Luckily there was not much crime in this normally quiet town, other than all the reporters still pestering them about the killing of the serial murderers. They still hounded Sarah when she tried to go shopping or take Van Gogh to the vet to check his injuries from the attack by Harcourt. Dave and his deputies had threatened them with arrest, but they all claimed their rights as the press to tell the world about the incident.

Dave just would force them to get back and life went on. This morning he was ready to go out as he kissed Sarah, still in bed. "Don't lounge there all day now, I'll be checking." He laughed and went off. Sarah rolled over and looked at the clock. She looked down to see Van Gogh staring at her by the side of the bed.

"What do you want, food or a crap?" she asked. Van Gogh barked and wagged his tail. "Okay, wait." She pulled herself out of bed and sat on the edge. Van Gogh went to the door and looked impatient. "Okay, hold on."

She stood and put on a robe, following the dog to the back door. Van Gogh was bouncing around as she opened the door and he ran out. "Don't take all day," she yelled.

Sarah dragged herself to the kitchen. She and Dave had remodeled it to be more user friendly towards Sarah. She was not a great cook, but Dave set up the kitchen to have all the appliances handy. The cupboards were organized so she could find anything she needed and quickly. Now the chore of fixing breakfast was on Sarah, since Dave was usually off to work early.

Bob Moats

She wasn't fond of cooking, but she needed sustenance in the morning so she learned to survive. Dave taught her how to make the great pancakes he had mastered. It took her a while, but she learned and was even able to flip them without hitting the ceiling, or the stove.

She let Van Gogh back in when she saw him bouncing at the back door, and then fed him. She ambled back to the bedroom, showered and dressed to face the world.

What she wanted was a good cup of coffee from Starbucks, but the nearest was over 200 miles away. So she brewed her own cup and took it to the living room. Dave had placed her desk by the big window so she could look out. Unfortunately it was not the great view she had in her last home. Back there she could look out and see the Hood Canal and the sea gulls sailing over the water. In this new home her view was of the long front yard, the main road into town and across the road, a cemetery.

She shivered every time she looked to the cemetery, so she usually tried not to look that far. She was determined to plant trees along the front of the property to block the view.

She sat at the desk, placing the coffee cup on a cup warmer and turned it on. She started up the laptop that held the chapters for the book that she was writing and took a sip of the coffee. It wasn't very tasty, but it provided her the needed caffeine to wake her up. The computer finally started up and she reread the last chapter she wrote.

Fatal Departure

She sat back and looked over to Van Gogh as he sat next to her chair. His eyes went from her to the laptop and back. "Don't you start badgering me to write. I don't know how these writers can get the motivation to do this. I've been on this for weeks and only have eight chapters done."

Van Gogh made his usual huffing noise that he made when he was bored. "Hey don't take that attitude with me. I'm going to write. I just need inspiration."

She looked out to the cemetery and shivered. "Okay that helped. Now on to murder." She sat forward and started to tap away at the keyboard as Van Gogh went off to lay down by the couch.

All the incidents about the serial killers were still fresh in her mind. The e-mails she had from Harcourt basically confessing to the murders he committed helped. Hal, her former boss at the publishing company she worked for, said if the book was good, he'd consider taking a shot at it. She was happy and still had a good deal of money from the insurance on her late husband, so they wouldn't starve.

The house on the canal still hadn't sold, so technically she still owned it. She didn't want to live there, after the murders in the living room, it was too creepy. Then she looked out the window. "Was that any creepier than living across from a cemetery?" she said to herself. Van Gogh lifted his head, stared and then went back to sleep.

She spent the next hour writing her story, trying to be as accurate as she could about what had happened. She would cringe when she added the gruesome facts about the murders of all the book editors. She found out from the

FBI who investigated Harcourt that he was killing editors and working his way across the country to Sarah. She also found out that he wanted to murder her because she rejected his manuscript years back. To carry a grudge all that time, he had to be a wacko, she thought.

She remembered how Harcourt sat in her living room with his throat slit open and shivered again. Then she looked up just as a hearse and a small procession was passing on its way to the cemetery. Not a sight to see this early in the morning. "Maybe I should go back to bed," she said to Van Gogh. He just snorted and continued sleeping.

*

Chapter 2

Dave was trying to get the fax machine to cooperate. He had one last report to send to the FBI in regards to the shootings in Sarah's old house. The crime would just not go away. The machine finally gave a whimper, grabbed onto each sheet of the papers and sent them. Dave turned to Virgil, his friend and the new deputy, and said, "We need to update our equipment. This stuff is out of the 80's. Have you heard from Mike?"

Virgil stood at his new desk and said, "He's coming in to work around four, he's been slacking off since he broke his leg. I think he's looking for sympathy."

Fatal Departure

"Well, he won't get any here. Have you been out on patrol at all this morning?"

"I pulled over two speeders going through town. No crime to report other than Abe Martin's mail box was given a whack again. We picked it up and put it back."

"Someone doesn't like that man. Maybe we'll have to put a stake out on it." Dave laughed.

"I'm not sitting out all night to catch some teenagers with a baseball bat. There are more important things to do."

"Like what Virgil? We have no crime to speak of and we spend more time sitting around the office, catching speeders or hanging at the Halfway House eating pastries and drinking coffee. Hell, the most excitement we've had in years was the serial killers."

"Yeah, I guess we have it easy. But a stake out on a mail box?"

"Be glad you have this job. I'll get you a nice thermos of coffee and a box of donuts to take on your stake out."

"You're serious about this?"

Dave was trying not to laugh out loud, "Don't worry, Virg, hopefully they will stop after last night. But if not, you will be watching."

"Deal, now I have to go put more gas in the cruiser." He said and left the office.

Dave sat at his desk when the phone rang. "Hello?"

"Sheriff Chandler?"

"Yes, may I help you?"

"I'm Special Agent Ron Trombley, FBI in the Seattle office; do you have a minute to talk?"

"I just sent out the last file on the case, didn't you get it?" he said looking to the fax, papers in the out tray.

"I'm not calling about that, it's someone else's case. I'm calling about intel that we received about possible trouble heading your way."

Dave paused waiting for more, nothing came. "And that would be?"

"We have been tracking crime in Seattle and there has been talk of a certain person coming your way."

"You've said that, just who is coming our way?"

"We are not sure, but there is trouble to be expected. This is just a heads up."

"Well, thank you Special Agent, I'll alert all my men to the situation," he said trying not to laugh.

"Very good, you have my number on your caller ID, let me know if you hear anything." He hung up.

"Now that was strange," he said.

Fatal Departure

"What was strange?" came a voice from behind him. Dave jumped slightly and turned to see Lois Carter standing at the counter.

"Lois, what brings you here?"

"I just wanted to let you know how the house showings have been going."

"And?"

"Well, the economy is still a bit shaky, so there have not been many people interested. Plus what the house is listed for, well… it's a bit high."

"It's what Sarah paid for it, in full. So do houses depreciate like cars?"

"No Dave, it's just people don't have the money now days."

"So why are they looking to buy a house? If they don't have money maybe they should rent. Like Sarah and I are doing with the shack you showed us."

"Shack? Dave, you guys loved the house when I first showed it to you."

"Sorry, I'm just a little annoyed that there are so many things wrong with it. Good thing we are only renting for now. The deal was, if the big house sells then we'd consider buying the shack. We've been having second thoughts, but we're waiting to see what happens."

"Dave, I'll do whatever it takes to make you guys happy. I have other properties I can show you, but Sarah was so anxious to get out of the big house, she agreed to move in."

"Yes, it was a speedy move, but it's not the end."

"And there's the other thing."

"Other thing?"

Lois paused, "I am bound by law and rules and have to inform prospective buyers that there were murders committed in the house. It's been tough to sell after that."

"Yeah, I understand that. I'm sorry if I'm being bitchy, I'm just having some concerns lately."

"You and Sarah aren't having second thoughts about being together?"

"No it's not that, she's having bad dreams about the murders. It's happen only twice now but I think it may happen again. I've mentioned to her about getting help, from Dr. Gladwin, but I think she may not want that help."

"Well, I think you can sway her into it. Doris Gladwin is a good therapist; she can help Sarah if no one else can."

"Thanks Lois, but don't you push her to it. Let me work on her, she can be stubborn."

"I'll back off trying to push her, for her own good, but do what you can to get her started."

Fatal Departure

"I will, thanks."

"Well, I have to be going, just wanted to let you know what was developing on the house. Sorry I have no good news." She gave a brave face and left.

Dave sat thinking on all that happened since Sarah came into town, and into his life. He was totally happy that he found Sarah, but the crime following her was not good. At least the killers were all gone, so hopefully she was safe. His life was busy now keeping Sarah happy and distracted from the horrible incident. She was doing better now, working on her story, and keeping in touch with her friend in New York, Connie. They were getting the bugs worked out of her story, Sarah writing, Connie editing. He hoped Sarah had no desire to murder her editor.

Dave heard the front door open and Sarah came around the corner with Van Gogh in tow.

"Well, this is pleasant? What are you doing here?" Dave asked.

"I had to get out, and Van Gogh wanted to take a ride. We turned at the wrong street and ended up here. Crazy huh?"

"I'd wouldn't say crazy. Are you thinking anything more about seeing Dr. Gladwin?"

"I don't know, do you think I may have more bad dreams?"

"It would be good to head it off, before it happens again. Oh and Lois just left."

"I know. I saw her car outside so I waited. I'm not up to seeing her now. Has she sold the house yet?"

"Still at it, economy is not cooperating. Besides the murders are a deal killer."

"She could just not mention it. She never mentioned the house alarms to me, so why is she telling people about the murders?"

"It's something that would come out eventually and Lois would get in trouble for not disclosing it. The alarms were a feature, the killings were not."

"I guess so. How's everything here? Is Virgil working out so far?"

"He's doing well, he does have some experience. He used to be a security guard in Tacoma. He went through the training, gun qualifying and everything required to be a deputy. So I'm happy."

"Sure, nepotistic hiring practices helped, too. Did the town council know?"

"Hell, half of them are related to Virgil. It wasn't hard to get him approved."

"So, want to get some fattening donuts at Halfway House?" she asked.

Fatal Departure

Dave seemed distracted, then looked down to his waistline and smiled. "I guess I can put on a few more pounds, let me call Virgil and tell him where I'll be, then we'll go." He reached for the radio and called Virgil in his car. He finished telling him about being at the restaurant and clicked off.

"Shall we go," he said to Sarah and the three of them left the office.

Dave put Van Gogh in the back of the patrol car and then he and Sarah got in the front. They drove to the restaurant and went in to a booth. Clara came bouncing up and said her spiel and went off to get water for them.

"I don't see any family resemblance to you, so I guess she's not your daughter."

"I told you, I had a brief thing with her mother years before she was born. Now drop it." Dave said sourly.

"Gee, I'm sorry for intruding. I was just trying to be light about it."

"Hey, I'm sorry; I just have my mind on something that's bugging me."

"Care to share it with a civilian?"

He paused and thought about the phone call earlier. "I got a call from an Agent in the FBI office in Seattle, it seemed strange. Not like an official call, very brief and vague. I'm wondering why and who actually called."

"Why don't you call the office there and inquire?"

"Gee, I didn't think of that. Maybe it's worth a few minutes to find out."

Clara came back with their waters and took their orders. They both decided on steak and eggs. Dave studied Clara's features and remembered her mother back when he and she were dating.

He smiled as Sarah said, "Get your mind out of the gutter and make a call to the FBI."

Dave gave her a grin and pulled his cell phone. He ran through his contact list and found the office in Seattle, he dialed. After a few rings someone answered and he asked for Agent Ron Trombley, the person on the other end took a moment to check and came back. Dave listened and then hung up.

He looked to Sarah and said, "Now I'm wondering, there is no agent by that name in the Seattle office, or anywhere in Washington State. This has me worried."

*

Chapter 3

Back in his office, Dave wrote down the phone number from his caller ID, that came in from the mysterious caller. He studied it for a moment; the area code was from the Seattle area, so that much was real.

Fatal Departure

"Are you going to call, or just sit there thinking about it?" Sarah said from the chair next to his desk.

"Give me a minute, I'm organizing my attack on this."

"By the time you're organized, I'll have grey hair."

Dave gave her a frown, then picked up the phone and dialed. The phone kept ringing on the other end, and then the voicemail female did her speech to leave a message. Dave hung up and sat back.

"No answer and the voicemail didn't give a name of the person on the other end. Makes me think it may be a throwaway phone. I'll call a friend in the FBI and give him the number, they can trace it better."

"Do you think it may be a prank? We've had all kinds of weirdos since this all started. Besides all the reporters, there have been a number of people who worship serial killers popping up. All of them turning my old house into a shrine."

"Yeah, it could be. Someone trying to give themselves a thrill, to see if they can shake up the police."

"Looks like it's working," Sarah said with a smile.

"Nothing shakes me up, I'm a calm and collected person."

"Too calm and collected, I think sometimes you should shake things up."

"I'll think about it."

"Again, calm and collected. Well, I should get back to writing, thank you for the food." She stood and kissed him just as Virgil came back in the building.

"Hey Sarah," he said with a grin.

"Hey Virgil," she replied, "I was just leaving, don't wake Dave up, he's being calm and collected."

Virgil gave her a puzzled look, as she laughed and went out with Van Gogh.

"She can be a bit odd sometimes," Virgil said, then went to his desk and sat.

"Odd more times than not, but don't say that to her. How much was the fill-up on the new cruiser?"

Virgil handed Dave the receipt from the gas station and Dave gave a small yelp as he looked at the price "Damn thing takes a lot doesn't it?"

"And the price of gas is way too high. Although I like this car better than that other antique we have."

"This one is the new police interceptor model; the other car was just one off the used car lot and painted to look like a cop car. We're lucky to get it to go over 60. Now, if I can talk the town council into buying us another one to replace the old one, it would be nice."

"I'll talk to Uncle Tim and see what he says."

21

Fatal Departure

Dave made no comment about his new deputy having relatives on the council, he just hoped it would get them what they needed.

Dave reached for the phone after hunting up the number of his friend in the FBI. He waited for an answer as he watched Virgil trying to make coffee on the antique Mr. Coffee machine that Dave had picked up at a yard sale. Dave thought it would be nice to update all their equipment. A talk with Uncle Tim might help.

"Hello, Special Agent Warren Stevens here, may I help you?"

"Warren, it's Dave Chandler. Got a minute?"

"Yo Dave, how the hell are you? I heard you took down some serial killers, pretty impressive."

"Just trying to get my name in the papers. I need a favor."

"Anything for the hero of the month; ask me."

"I got a call this morning from some guy claiming to be an FBI agent. He gave me a warning about trouble coming my way. I checked with the Seattle office and was told he doesn't exist. I have a name and the phone number he gave me, can you check it?"

"Pretending to be a FBI agent is a federal offense. Give me what you got and I'll see what I can find."

"The number he gave went to voicemail and nothing else. Got a pencil?"

"Shoot." Dave gave him the name and number and then his friend said, "I'll see what we can find and get back to you. Do you think it's someone yanking your chain or something worse? A warning from some psycho? Your high profile case was big news, lots of nuts can be attracted to it."

"Are you a behavioral profiler now?" Dave laughed.

"I'm trying to get my degree in Psych to maybe move up. It's better than getting shot at by some psycho."

"Well, do your profile on this guy and let me know."

"I hear you're shacking up with the woman who the killer went after."

"Nothing slips your attention, does it? Yes, we are living together for now. She's quite a woman, better than the bitch I was living with. She's in Seattle now, ever run into her?"

"Which one, Farrah or Linda? I've lost track of your conquests."

"Farrah, she moved there about four months ago."

"I'll watch out for her, as I remember she was hot."

"Yes, and she'll burn you good. I'm still scarred from the fire. Find out what you can on the call and get back with me."

Fatal Departure

"Will do, buddy. Talk later." He hung up and Dave stood. He went to get some of the coffee, now that the machine had finally finished spitting out the murky brew.

"Coffee is lousy, drink at your own risk," Virgil said.

Dave took a sip and made a face. "I'm going to the restroom to pour this down the drain. Then I'm going to go out and get some real coffee. Hold down the fort."

"Cream and two sugars," Virgil yelled to Dave as he was leaving.

~~*~~

Sarah was back at her computer staring at the screen. Van Gogh was watching her from the floor where he had plopped down, then snorted.

"Don't snort at me, I'm trying to remember the incidents that happened. I'd be glad for your help in writing this, if you think you can do better."

Her desk phone rang causing her to jump. She composed herself and answered, "Hello?"

"Sarah, this is your editor, where are your chapters?"

"Connie! I'm working on them right now, so don't you start bugging me too," she replied with a laugh.

"Too? Who else is bugging, Dave?"

"No, Van Gogh is giving me the eye as I sit here."

"The dog is giving you the stink eye? Well, it's good someone is. How's life in the woods?"

"Boring, but I can look to the cemetery across the road for comfort."

"Why did you guys move there anyways?"

"I was in a rush to get out of the house of crime, and this place wasn't bad, other than the cemetery. I think Dave and I may look more, this place needs too much work done to it."

"You two could move to New York and leave all the "Green Acres" life behind," Connie laughed.

"Actually I'm enjoying life here, but it could change. Although Dave is a fixture here, he likes being Sheriff. So I don't see any long distance moves in our immediate future."

"Whenever, just send me something good to read. Hal is driving me nuts with all the submissions that are coming in."

"Well, don't sign your name to any of the rejects. You don't need a killer coming for you, too," Sarah warned.

"I won't, take care and we'll talk later when I'm out of the office." She hung up and Sarah put the phone down. She jumped when she saw Van Gogh standing next to her.

"I suppose you want to go out? I need to put a doggy door in the back, then you can go out whenever you please. But if I did, you'd probably bring in all your little animal friends."

She got up and went to the back door, opened it and let the dog out. She turned to the kitchen and poured out the dry dog food, just to get ahead of Van Gogh. She went back to the computer as a thought came into her head and wanted to put it in the story before she forgot it. She worked on it for a while longer, let Van Gogh in and then went to check her e-mail.

Thankfully nothing from disgruntled writers. She stopped doing all editing for others after she found out the reason for Harcourt's attack. She didn't like editing her own chapters, so she asked Connie to help. It allowed her to concentrate on the story and not the grammar. She worked for a little longer, then went to take a nap. Van Gogh followed her to the bedroom and she let him come up with her on the bed.

~~*~~

Across the road, in the cemetery, a hole was being dug. It would be filled later with the remains of another citizen of Jefferson County, where the town was situated. The two men, who were busy digging in the dirt, were talking about the latest sports scores. They were not paying attention to a figure standing away from them behind a tall tombstone, watching. He waited until they were finished. The two grave diggers left and the man went to the fresh hole and looked down. He smiled, looked around for anyone in the cemetery, and then went to his car parked nearby. He opened the trunk and carefully pulled out a large plastic bag and took it to the hole. He dumped the bag into the hole and picked up one of the shovels and proceeded to cover the bag. He figured that the hole was deep enough so people wouldn't realize it wasn't as deep as before. He made sure that the bag was covered, then went back to his car, and drove off.

*

Chapter 4

It was a very large library; the shelves went up twenty feet easily, ladders standing by, to reach the top heights. She walked between the stacks and marveled at all the books, then she heard a noise. It was a thudding sound, like a foot dropping hard on a wood floor. She turned to look back and then the lights went out. The only light now was the moon shining through the skylights above. She heard the thud again and it frightened her. She tried to find the exit, but was going round and round in the aisles of books, all shaking on the shelves. The noise they made gave her a fright, she ran faster to get away from the now twitching books. They slid in and out around her and she ducked to avoid being hit in the head, as they started flying out at her.

She came out of the stacks and found herself standing by the long desks of the library. It was still dark but she could see three figures coming slowly towards her. She couldn't make out who they were, but they wanted her for her blood. She knew this, somehow. They came towards her, closer, as she looked for an opening to escape, but saw none. Suddenly a door opened to her right, light blazing in. She could see the three figures clearly now, they had the flesh falling off their faces and their skulls showed through. She ran for the door where she saw a man in a police uniform standing in the opening.

She felt safe, but when she reached him, he too was grotesque, flesh melting off his face. She screamed, loudly.

"Okay, that's it. Wake up Sarah." Dave called gently to her as he held on to her tightly. She looked up to him, still in his sheriff's uniform. She glanced to the clock by the bed and it said almost three o'clock, light shining through the window, it was still afternoon.

"I just got home, and was in the kitchen when I heard you scream. You were taking a nap, and you had a bad dream again," he said, "Now, will you go see the doctor?"

She wiped the tears from her cheeks and quietly said, "Yes."

Dave had changed into his civilian clothing as Sarah sat at her desk. She sat staring at the screen of her computer, not moving. Dave came into the room and went to her.

"Maybe re-living the murders through your book is bringing on the dreams?" he said.

"I haven't written about that part of it, I'm on the crimes Harcourt committed on his way across the country."

"Well, it's still bringing back the bad thoughts. Maybe you could put the book aside for a while until you talk to Dr. Gladwin, ' he said.

She didn't reply, she just watched the computer screen saver moving around. Then she said, "Maybe you're right. I'll think on it."

"I'm sure you'll do what you feel is right. Now let's get out of here and go get a nice dinner somewhere."

"Not the Halfway House, please. Can we have a good sit down dinner complete with waiters and busboys?"

"You got it, there's the Blue Goose restaurant down the 101, how's that sound?"

"Never been in there, I guess it sounds good."

They gathered themselves together and left Van Gogh in the house. The restaurant was nice and they had a great meal with good service. They went back home and it was now about nine, Dave was tired and had to work the next morning so he went off to bed. Sarah said she couldn't sleep right now, so she went to her computer and worked on her book a while. She didn't know exactly when she fell asleep in her chair, but she had no bad dreams.

Her head suddenly snapped up when she heard the loud crash. Lightning flashed through the front window, startling her. She looked to her desk clock, it was two-nineteen. Then the rains came. She stood and went to the window, watching the storm brewing outside in the dark.

Fatal Departure

She didn't mind storms, just not being out in one. Every time the lightning flashed she could see the cemetery across the road, her skin crawled. She thought about being underground in a coffin, while rain seeped all around you. She knew she wouldn't be alive, but she just hated the thought of drowning in a coffin. That actually made her smile, she was being silly.

She went into the bedroom, followed by a droopy looking Van Gogh. She undressed and crawled under the covers. Thunder struck again, she could see the lightning through the bedroom window. She snuggled up to Dave, he put his arm around her and said sleepily, "I'll protect you from the storm."

She giggled and kissed him, turning on her side to sleep again. Hopefully with no bad dreams.

Six o'clock rolled around and Dave was up getting ready for the day. Sarah stretched out in the space vacated by Dave.

"Don't get too comfortable there. I'm going to call Dr. Gladwin and set up an appointment for you. When is a good day?"

"How about next month?" she said with a grin.

"Next week, either Monday or Tuesday. That will give you three days to see if you have any more bad dreams." Dave went to the bedroom window and looked out. "Rain stopped about two hours ago, but it sure soaked everything. Don't goof around now, I'll see you later."

He went out the bedroom door and she could hear him go out the back door. Then he started up his Bronco and drove out. She sat up in bed as Van Gogh jumped up and plopped down at her feet.

"Shall we get some work done today? We need groceries, so get up and out of the bed." Van Gogh stood and jumped down, looking back to her by the door. "Give me a minute, please. I don't move as fast as you. And I have to put on clothes, you're so lucky to be able wear the same outfit all the time." She did her ritual of getting ready and then went to the kitchen grabbing pencil and paper.

She checked her supplies and wrote down what she would need. She let Van Gogh do a quick potty run then took him to the Vibe and drove out the long drive. She went to the Brinnon General Store, it was a small store with gas pumps in front, but it had the necessary items she needed. She missed the big box stores, like WalMart and KMart. Once every two weeks, she and Dave would run down to Olympia and stock up on important things, like toilet paper in jumbo bags.

Van Gogh was watching patiently in the car as Sarah brought out the two bags of groceries they would need to get them through the week. She stood looking at the road as a funeral procession passed, heading to her favorite cemetery. Now she would get stuck behind them as they inched along the highway.

She decided to go visit Dave first, giving time for the procession to reach their destination. She put the groceries in the back of the small car and climbed in. She arrived at the Sheriff's office and saw both patrol cars were gone. She put Van Gogh on his short leash and went in.

"Hi Mike, how's the leg?" she asked the young deputy, who broke his leg back when the killers were in town.

"I'm good, Sarah. Hey Van Gogh, are you being a good dog?" he asked with a laugh.

Van Gogh wagged his tail and yipped.

"Where's Dave?" Sarah asked.

"Oh, uh… he and Virgil are out at the cemetery. They got a call about a hour ago, that they found a body."

"Mike, there are lots of bodies in the cemetery," she said.

"Yes, but this one wasn't supposed to be there. It was put in a hole dug for a funeral this morning. The rain storm last night put enough water in the hole to flood it, it wasn't covered up properly, and the cemetery people had to pump the water out. Something got clogged in the pipe they used to pump the water out, and they pulled it up finding a big piece of plastic bag. One of the workers went down in the hole and found the remains of someone, who was not supposed to be there. They called us and Dave went out with Virgil."

"Well, that's comforting to know, are they stacking up bodies now? Saving space?" she was joking but the deputy wasn't laughing. "Sorry."

"That's okay, we don't get much excitement around here, well, except your excitement. Now we have a body dumped and that's not normal."

"I'm sure it isn't." She got a chill now thinking about a body turning up. She may as well be living back in New York. "Thanks Mike, tell Dave I stopped by."

"I'll do that, take care. So long Van Gogh, be a good dog." Van Gogh yipped again and followed Sarah out.

She sat in her car after she put Van Gogh in. "I'm not liking this, puppy," she said to the dog. "Too soon after my crime incident. This doesn't work well for me." She started the car and drove out. She went to the cemetery and drove through the rusty, tall, open entrance gates with a metal sign saying, "Jefferson County Cemetery".

She felt the chill again, but drove through. She saw the funeral procession waiting by the open grave as Dave, Virgil and three cemetery workers were busy handling what was left of the plastic bag and the remains of the body. They had called in the county coroner and his black van sat next to the hearse, making it twice as creepy. The M.E. put the body on a gurney and shoved it in the van.

Dave was standing, looking around when he saw Sarah. He came over as she rolled down the window. "How did you know I was here?"

"Mike told me, I stopped to see you. He told me what they found, who was the body?"

He paused, thinking about whether or not to tell her, then said, "We don't know yet, all we found was a torso and legs. The head and arms are missing."

She felt a chill and shivered again.

*

Chapter 5

"Do you think they'll be able to identify the body?" Sarah asked.

"I'm sure the coroner will figure it out, I hope." Dave replied.

"Well, there are less than 1,200 people in this town, do a door to door search and see who's missing." She smiled.

"Thanks for making my life miserable enough. Now, why don't you get out of here, I'll see you back home. I still have to calm the mourners about this being a crime scene. They may have to move the deceased to another spot and it could get ugly." He leaned in and kissed her. She started the car and drove off.

He stood watching her drive away, thinking how much she has gone through. This crap wasn't helping her frame of mind. He would need to talk to Doris Gladwin before he makes the appointment. Just to pick her brain for what he can do to help her. He went back to the plot to see what he could do to make everyone happy.

Sarah drove out from the cemetery to Church Road, and arrived at the house. She pulled into the drive and parked. Opening the door, Van Gogh jumped out and she pulled the groceries from the car and took them to the kitchen. After she put everything away, she went to her desk, sitting, and fired up her computer. She had two e-mails, one from Connie, with her corrections for the last chapter she sent, and one from some reporter asking for an interview. She wondered how they got her e-mail address. It was a personal account for her book business.

She read the e-mail, it was brief, "Dear Mrs. Keller, I'm Terry Buscemi, and I'd like to talk with you about the serial killings that you endured. I am a writer for the Seattle Sun Times and we would appreciate your input on the crimes. Please call me at 360-555-9834\ and I can make time to talk. Thank you, Terry."

Brief and to the point. Now she would have to change her e-mail address, or she would get all the nut jobs bugging her. She looked to the window and saw people moving around in the cemetery. Poor Dave she thought, having to keep the grief stricken family appeased.

She read the corrections Connie sent and worked on the chapter. She was happy that the book was going well. Hal did tell her he would take a shot at it, so maybe she would become famous as an author. Maybe she should do the interview, she could promote her forthcoming book that way. She opened up the e-mail again and wrote down the number.

Fatal Departure

She reached for the phone and called, it rang and a female voice answered, "Hello, Terry Buscemi speaking. May I help you?"

Sarah always hated when people were given ambiguous names that could be male or female, it could be confusing.

"Ms. Buscemi, I'm Sarah Keller, you sent me an e-mail about an interview?"

"Oh, Mrs. Keller, thank you for calling. Would you be open to an interview about the serial killers?"

"You do know I'm writing a book about it?"

"I've heard that."

"Well, I'll only agree to the interview if I can promote my book."

There was silence, then, "I see no problem, we can work it into the interview subtly."

"I need to know something, just how did you get my e-mail address. It's private."

"I'm sorry, I won't share it with anyone, and I won't use it again. I have some friends back in New York who work in publishing. They did some checking and came up with it. From your own publisher. I hope I wasn't intruding."

"Well, I try to keep it private. I'll let it go, but delete it from your address book. And I need to talk to my publisher about my privacy. Now how do you want to do the interview?"

"You tell me, I'm open. Would you like to do it in Brinnon, I can come up or we can meet wherever you want?"

"Where are you located?"

"Actually, I live in Olympia, even though I write for the Seattle Sun. I'm more of an outside Seattle reporter. I write about happenings around the area. I was hoping that if I could get an interview with you, it would give me some credibility with the newspaper."

Sarah figured she was some society news reporter looking for a big scoop. Well, if it does some good for her book, why not give the woman a chance for a little recognition. "I think you should come up here. We can talk at the Halfway House Restaurant on, say Tuesday, next week at noon." Sarah figured if she was any good, she'd find the place.

"That would be great, I'll be there. Thank you for this, I appreciate it."

"Okay, we'll talk then," she said and hung up. She sat back and looked out the front window, seeing Dave's Bronco coming up the drive. She stood and went to the kitchen and waited for him to come in. Van Gogh stood nearby waiting also.

The door opened and he came in, saw her and smiled. "Were you waiting for me?"

Fatal Departure

"I saw you drive in."

"Gee, I figured I'd catch you napping and attack you in bed," he said with an evil grin.

"Don't let my being here in the kitchen stop you," she said and went off towards the bedroom. Dave followed, but told Van Gogh to stay in the kitchen. Van Gogh just snorted and went back to the living room and jumped up on the couch.

About an hour later, they laid together in bed, holding each other. "You know we don't make love as often as we used to. You have to get up so early and to bed early. I think you should change jobs." Sarah said into his ear.

"Doing what?" he asked.

"I'm sure the Halfway House could use a good breakfast cook. How's that sound?"

"Not really inspiring. Would you give up your words and work at the General Store bagging groceries?"

"No, I guess not. Oh, by the way, I have an interview next week for the Seattle Sun. I talked to the reporter today and she is coming out. I'm going to promote my book and give her an interview."

"That's good, and I'll get you an appointment for Dr. Gladwin next week also."

"Gladwin, that's some name for a head shrinker, hi I'm Glad to Win, can you win too? Relax on the couch and tell me about your childhood."

"Don't make fun, she has helped a number of people in town, from mental health problems to marriage counseling."

"Did you and your former cupcake go to talk to her before the cupcake moved away?"

"Don't call her a cupcake, she was more of a fruitcake," he said and started to laugh, then he rolled over on her and started to kiss her.

"You are such a bad boy," she said and they went at it again.

Around another hour later, they came out of the bedroom and Van Gogh jumped off the couch as soon as he heard the door open. Dave went to the bathroom and Sarah went to the kitchen. She looked into the refrigerator and pulled out the two steaks she bought earlier. She pulled out the broiling pan and prepared the meat for cooking. Dave came in and marveled at her attempt to cook.

They had a nice meal, then went to the living room and sat on the couch. "Don't do any work on your story tonight. Let's just watch some mindless television and relax for once." Dave said.

"That's good for me," she replied and picked up the remote, turning on the TV and they settled in watching CSI, as Dave commented on the fictional police work.

They finished their mindless entertainment and shut off the TV, going to bed. Both tired from the day and the sex marathon they had gone through. They just held each other as Sarah asked, "How did you resolve the burial plot problem?"

"The funeral director talked to the cemetery people and got the burial moved to a crypt. That pleased the family, since it was more expensive, but not for them. The cemetery people were negligent in not covering up the hole and preventing a body dump, they wanted to avoid a lawsuit. So the crypt was a better solution."

"It would be nice if all people could handle their problems by agreeing."

"Yes, it would. But people usually are not very cooperative. It took a lot of negotiating today to keep everyone happy."

"Any word on your body?"

"None so far, but the torso had a small tattoo on the posterior..."

"You mean the ass?" Sarah said interrupting.

"Yes, the ass, thank you for correcting me. Anyway, we may be able to identify the body by the tattoo. I have Virgil checking tattoo parlors within a hundred miles of here."

"Well, that may turn up an answer. What was the tat of?"

"Tat? I presume you mean tattoo. We're not in New York, so we don't use all the fancy terms they do. The tattoo… as we call it out here in the boonies… was an odd symbol, like one of those hazard waste symbols. Not something one would burn into their ass."

She looked up to him and said, "Maybe he was a garbage man, you could check on that with your waste management people."

"I don't think so, not many people are so devoted to picking up garbage that they would tattoo it to their bodies. I think it was some tree hugger, environmental nut. But we won't know for a few days. Oh, and the M.E. said he died of a broken neck. Don't know why the head and arms were missing."

"Well, I'm going to sleep and if I dream about floating heads, I'm coming after you." Sarah said and rolled over.

*

Chapter 6

Dave checked in early at the office, putting Mike and Virgil in charge. He left and drove out to a small building on the western outskirts of town. The small sign on the gate said, "Dr. Doris Gladwin, PhD, Therapy and Counseling". He pushed the gate open and went up to the brick and wooden framed building. It was an older place, formerly a medical doctor's office, but when the new medical clinic opened on the south end of town the previous doctor moved there.

Fatal Departure

He approached the door as it opened and out came a svelte, attractive, brunette about five-ten and dressed professionally. "Dave, I saw you coming up. It's good to see you again. What can I do for you, as if I didn't know," she said crisply.

"What exactly do you know Doris?" he replied.

"Well, with all the excitement from the murders, I figured someone would need counseling. Is it Sarah?"

"You are good, or just well-schooled to know who needs help the most."

"I'm both," she laughed, "Come in won't you and we'll talk."

"Am I going to be charged for this?" Dave said with a grin.

"Dave, if I charged you, you'd just get it back by giving me tickets. Come in, it's free."

They went into the building and through the small anteroom, into a comfy office. She motioned to a chair and asked him to sit.

"Don't you have a couch I can recline on?"

"No, I'd get into trouble with a couch in here and the number of men I treat. I stopped with the couch thing long ago. Just comfortable easy chairs now. So tell me, what it is you need?"

"Well... it is Sarah. She's having really bad dreams lately. I've convinced her to come see you, just to see if you can help her get past the murders."

"I understand she's writing a book about the crimes, don't you think that is affecting her dreams?"

"I think it might be, but words are her life, she has her heart set on writing about this. At first I thought it would be good therapy - to bring out the crimes in her book, but the dreams make me wonder now."

"It's good that she is facing the incident by writing about it. But she must have been terribly scarred emotionally by the attack from the killers."

"She was a wreck for about a week after, then she started to heal. I did my best to keep her happy. She gave up her editing job in New York; she distanced herself from that life, and then she started on the book that she's determined to write."

"It can be good therapy, but I won't know until I talk to her. You said she's agreeable to come in?"

"Reluctantly, but yes, she's willing."

"Is she okay with you making an appointment for her?"

"I've already mentioned either Monday or Tuesday, she didn't disagree."

Fatal Departure

"Good, I don't work on weekends," she looked to a book on her desk, "I do have an opening on Monday, at one in the afternoon."

"I'll pass that to her, and probably give her a police escort here," he said with a laugh.

"Well, it's better if she comes willingly. So tell her I'll see her then." She stood as her door opened and a young woman put her head in. "Lilly, just wait a moment as I finish up here. The girl said nothing, backed out and closed the door. "My first patient of the day, good to see you again Dave."

Dave stood, said good-bye and left. Now he had to get Sarah into a mood to keep the appointment. He didn't want her to have any more bad dreams, but if she did, it may help to get her to talk to the Doctor. He went back to the patrol car and drove back to his office.

He parked and entered the building, Mike was at his desk. "Dave, you got a call from some guy in the FBI, he said he was a friend of yours. Call him back, the number is on your desk."

"Thanks Mike, I already have his number." He went to his desk and sat, picking up his phone and dialed. The phone rang a couple times and then his friend, Warren, answered. "Dave here, I'm back, what do you have on the phone call?"

"Well, this Ron Trombley was an FBI agent, but disappeared two years ago. So, you had a ghost call you, or he's still around. I've put a notice out in the bureau to be on the lookout for him. That number you gave me was a burn phone, it's now dead. So I don't have an answer for you, sorry."

"That was more than enough. Do you think it was Trombley, or someone impersonating him?"

"Tough call, I don't know why he would suddenly reappear and call you with a lame story about trouble coming your way. Unless he's the trouble. I've pulled his file and he is from Tacoma, you lived there with Farrah didn't you?"

"Yes I did, but I don't remember him. I was on the PD there for about two years before I got the offer to be sheriff here.

"Did Farrah have anything going with men before you?"

"Hell, she dated half of the men and a few women in Tacoma before we met. Trombley could have been one of them. But why bother me now, since I don't live with her anymore?"

"I'm not a profiler… yet, maybe you need to contact Farrah and see if there is a connection."

"Could you look her up? I don't really want to see her again. She left town without so much as a thank you for the sex," Dave said with a loud laughed. "Not that the sex was all that great with her."

"I'll take a stab at it, contacting her - not the sex."

Fatal Departure

"She'll probably pull you in. You're still good looking, aren't you?"

"Hell, no one is better looking than I am. Okay, I'll see what I can do and call you. Any words you want me to pass to her?"

"Nothing I would say to a lady, but she's no lady. Good luck."

"Talk later, buddy. Don't get shot," he said and hung up.

Dave sat back and watched Mike shooting rubber bands at the flies in the room. He shook his head and wondered why he kept Mike on. Probably because he worked cheap and was a cousin of the Mayor. Dave was the only person on the sheriff's team who wasn't related to someone in the town government. He wondered how he even got the job.

"Mike, why don't you take a car out and see how many tourists you can pull over for speeding." Dave finally said.

"Hey, that would be nice, I'll get on it," he said and left the room.

Dave smiled and picked up his phone, dialing Sarah at home. "Hey babe," he said when she answered, "I talked to Dr. Gladwin today, she's agreeable to meet with you Monday at one. Are you still okay with this?"

He waited for her to say something, then, "Yeah, I'll go and talk to her. How much is this going to cost me?"

"It will cost you your sanity, that's worth it, right?"

She paused again, "Yes it is. I'll be there, but you'll have to tell me where."

"I'll give you all the details later. What are you doing?"

"I'm sitting here trying to write, but I'm blocked."

"Babe, the crime was real, you don't have to make it up. It happened and all you have to do is write it down. Am I correct?"

She paused again, "Okay, I know what I have to write, but it's hard to do it. I'm thinking I may put this book away for now. At least until I get over my bad dreams."

"And Dr. Gladwin should be able to help with that, go see her and then decide if you want to put the book away. Just let it rest until Monday. See what happens. Let's have a weekend with no murders, okay?"

"Deal. When are you coming home?"

Dave looked at the clock on the wall, it was just before Noon. "I still have about four hours to work. How about lunch at the Halfway House, my treat?"

"I'll meet you there."

Fatal Departure

"Let me call Virgil back in from his patrol and I'll be there in about twenty minutes." She agreed and they hung up. Dave reached for the radio and called Virgil.

The Halfway House was busy as Dave came in and saw Sarah sitting with Lois. Great, he thought. He went to them and sat next to Sarah. "Hello Lois. How are you?"

"I'm good Dave. I have someone interested in the house. They are from Arizona and thinking about moving here. He's retired and loves fishing. I told him the Hood Canal has great fishing. They will be coming up next week to take a look."

"Have you told him about the murders?" Sarah asked.

"Yes, I did. He's a retired police officer from Flagstaff and he doesn't care. It looks good."

"Well, let us know," Dave said. Clara came up with the waters, took their orders and went off.

"Lois, if the house sells, we need to see a few more houses. The one we're in is not the best, it needs too much work and the cemetery is not something we need to live across from." Dave said.

Dave's cell phone rang and he pulled it out. "Hello?" He listened and then hung up. "Sorry ladies, I have to leave. Another body has turned up."

*

Chapter 7

The dirt road just off the 101 north of town led out to the Hood Canal. At the end of what became more of a trail, it dead-ended just before the water, where Dave could see Virgil and two men standing by a black plastic bag. Dave pulled up alongside of the new police cruiser, parked next to a pickup truck. He got out and went to the men waiting for him.

"Okay, what's the story?" Dave asked.

Virgil cleared his throat and said, "This is Harvey and Elwood Downy. They come out here to fish and found this." He pointed to the thing as Dave knelt down to the partially opened bag. He could see an arm attached to the torso. "Did you call the M.E.?"

"I did, they're' on the way. I think there are no legs this time, by the shortness of the bag. Oh, and still no head."

"I see that." He turned to the men and asked. "Was the body right here when you found it?"

One of the men, an older one by his gray hair, said, "Just right there, Sheriff. I opened the bag to see what it was. Sometimes people dump their garbage along the shore, I wanted to make sure what it was. I ain't ever seen a dead person before… well, except at a funeral, but not on the shore."

"Glad you called, I presume you have a cell phone?"

49

Fatal Departure

"Sure do, I wouldn't be out here without one. I'm have a problem with my ticker, the heart I mean, and I need to be able to call for help, if need be."

"Okay, Virgil move them carefully away from the crime scene and take their formal statement and they can go. Thank you gentlemen." Dave went back to his patrol car and sat. He reached for the radio and called Mike back in the station.

"Yeah Dave," Mike said answering the call.

"Mike get on the phone and call the State Police and get their forensic people out here. We've probably messed up the crime scene by walking all over it, but maybe they can still find something."

"Will do Dave. Oh, and you had a call from your FBI friend again. I told him I'd pass a message along."

Dave waited, then asked, "What was the message, Mike?"

"Oh, yeah, sorry. He said that he found Farrah and she doesn't know the man you guys are looking for. He did say to tell you Farrah is still a knock out."

"I really needed to hear that," he said with a smile. "Okay, make the call, I'll have Virgil wait here for them."

They signed off and he sat looking at the bag, still flat out on the ground. "What's going on here? Are serial killers making this their dumping ground now?" he said to himself. He got out of the car, as the two men were getting in their truck and leaving. Dave went to Virgil, "Make sure you write out the report and when the state police forensic people get here, get their report too."

"You want me to wait out here for them?" he asked, looking nervously to the body, like it was going to attack him.

"Yes, Virgil. You can just sit in your nice, shiny new car and wait. Make sure the M.E. tells you anything he discovers about the body and put it in your report. I have to go back to the office and call the FBI. We may have a serial killer on our hands again."

"That's not good," Virgil said.

"No it's not, so be on the alert. I get the feeling this is not the end of it." Dave went back to his car and drove out, leaving Virgil all alone.

Dave stopped at the junction of the dirt road and the 101, looking around at the area. It would be easy to drive out here, drop the bag and take off. But where did the killer come from? Was this person a resident or an outsider? If he was an outsider, was he staying at one of the motels? He thought he'd check out the motels and see who may be around. He was getting ready to drive out and back into town, when he heard something move in his back seat.

~~*~~

Sarah managed to get through lunch with Lois. Luckily, Lois didn't stay long and Dave gave Sarah money for the food before he left. She got the takeout box of

Fatal Departure

Dave's lunch and then realized she didn't have a car. She came with Dave and she was suddenly struck with the realization that Van Gogh was missing. She pulled her cell to called Dave. Before she could call, she felt a hand on her shoulder. She looked up and it was Dave.

"Van Gogh suddenly startled me from the back seat where he was sleeping all the time I was gone. I realized that I had left you stranded here with Lois. I'm sorry." He sat in the booth and took his doggy box and removed the burger from it. "Still warm at least," he laughed.

"So what happened?" she asked.

"Well, same M.O., dumped black plastic bag with a body, missing parts. This time the legs and still the head." He said between bites of the burger.

"Maybe Dr. Frankenstein is in town and collecting parts to make another monster. Alert the townspeople to get their torches and pitchforks ready." She said with a grin.

Dave was relieved that she was joking about it. He worried that with what happened to her, this would be a problem.

"If this person is cutting up the bodies, where would he do it and how? Did you hear from the M.E. as to how the parts were cut off the body?" Sarah asked.

"You seem to know something about this," he said chewing the burger.

"Remember, I edited many crime novels. I should be a deputy too, I have the experience, even if it was on paper."

"I'll get you a badge and you can be a civilian adviser. It would be better than Mike or Virgil trying to solve the case. I hate to say it, but between the two of them, they have just enough brain power to light a candle."

Sarah laughed. Dave thought it sounded nice. She hadn't been overly happy lately, with all the dreams.

"I have to go back to the office and call the FBI, to let them know we may have a..." he paused, thinking.

"You can say it, serial killer. I figured that from the first body. My dreams may be messed up, but I'm still together about this. And I've read this plot before in books. Nothing is new."

"Well if you read about this, who did it? You can save us a lot of time running around."

"I didn't say the crimes I read were exactly like this, but some of the plots are the same. There's not much new under the sun. You still have to investigate, but I'll help."

"I'll take that under advisement and get back to you."

"Don't make light of this, I have a good mind for solving things. You should see me do the New York Times crossword puzzle."

53

Fatal Departure

"Okay, I'll throw things to you and see how you do. Does that work for you?"

"Perfectly. Now that you polished off that burger, shall we go call the FBI?" Sarah said with a grin.

Dave stood and smiled. They went out to let Van Gogh take a quick run before going back to the office.

~~*~~

He sat by the window in the restaurant watching the sheriff and the woman talking in their booth, then leaving. He paid his bill, then went to this car, sitting for a moment to study the map of the area. He was marking off the places where he put the black plastic bags and circled places to put more. He wasn't taking chances with people missing from the town, so he would drive down to Olympia, find a street person or homeless man for his little presents. He started the car and went to the small building he was renting from an out of town owner he found through the Seattle Sun ads. He drove around the back and parked. The building was secluded, surrounded by trees and brush that hid it from the road. Or prying eyes.

He entered the building, it was sparsely furnished, a cot, table, chairs, small refrigerator - all in one room. He went to the door off the left, opened it, and went in. It was dark, he turned on the lights. In front of him was a long low table covered with a plastic drop cloth. The floor was cover with plastic also. He sorted through the various tools on a side table. There was a surgical saw, various knives and a hacksaw. All ready to carve up another victim. He was determined to give Sheriff Chandler so many bodies, he would be overwhelmed by them. Bastard, he thought.

~~*~~

Mike was by the front counter talking to a woman, complaining about the noise her neighbor's teens were making. Mike was writing it all down as Dave came in followed by Sarah with Van Gogh.

"Hello Mrs. Danforth. What's the concern now?" Dave asked the woman.

"Noisy teens. They should be locked up. And driving crazy at night. You really need to watch them."

"We'll give them a warning and if they break the law, they will be punished. Thank you for your concern." He said and went to this desk.

The woman looked to Van Gogh and said, "Is that dog dangerous? He should have a muzzle."

Sarah said "Well, maybe the muzzle should be...", but Dave coughed and gave her a look, she stopped and just smiled.

*

Chapter 8

It took three rings before Special Agent Warren Stevens answered, "Dave, I want to thank you for having me look up Farrah."

"Don't start and if you get hurt, don't blame me. Now let's be serious, I need help. We have what is shaping up to be a serial killer. Can you send someone or come down yourself to give us some help?"

"Talk to me, in detail," he said. Dave spent a couple of minutes covering the body dumps. Warren was quiet for too long, then he said, "Black plastic bags with body parts missing, eh? You have a problem, Dave. Like the mysterious Ron Trombley said, trouble is coming your way."

"Can you not be you and talk like a real FBI agent?" Dave asked.

"Okay, we had a serial killer here about two years ago. He dropped bodies or partial bodies around the Seattle area, all wrapped up in plastic bags. We never caught him and he murdered over 20 people, mostly homeless. We got close to him a couple times and then he managed to grab the lead Detective on the case. We found him murdered two days later. He had a note pinned to his chest... no shirt, just pinned to his flesh. It said that he exacted his revenge on the Detective. Why the revenge, we don't know. Have you pissed off anyone?"

Bob Moats

"I piss off a lot of people, sometimes not even deliberately. But none big enough to be pulling this crap. Can you come down… and leave Farrah up there?"

Warren laughed, "I'll talk to my supervisor and see what we can set up. If this is the same guy, I know there are a lot of friends of the murdered Detective, who'd like to get their hands on him. Let me get back to you, and watch your back," he laughed and before he hung up he said, "Oh, and I didn't like the way Farrah had turned out, so she's not on my date list." He hung up and Dave thought on what he had said about the serial killer.

Sarah was sitting patiently and then asked, "So what did he say?"

Dave came out of his thoughts, then he told Sarah about the serial killer in Seattle. She was quiet all through his explanation and then frowned.

"I'm not liking this, if he is coming after you. It was bad enough when I was the target of a killer, but I won't stand for you being the source of attraction."

Dave smiled, leaned forward, and kissed her, then said, "I'll be careful, and so will you. I'm putting a body guard on you 24/7."

"Like hell you are, I have Van Gogh to protect me."

"Has he been pumping up? We'll take this one day at a time. Maybe we'll be able to solve this quickly."

Fatal Departure

"Well, I'm going home to write, I'm getting inspired by all this crime. Come on Van Gogh, we have work to do." She stood, kissed him and took the dog out to he car.

Dave looked to Mike and said, "We have a problem, and we need to make a plan. See if Virgil is done at the murder scene and we'll put our heads together." He stood and went to the restroom, as Mike called Virgil.

~~*~~

Sarah arrived home, went to the drawer where Dave kept an extra service revolver, checked it to be sure it was ready to fire and put it back. She wasn't going to take chances. She went to the computer and worked on her book. It was quiet in the house, Van Gogh was on the floor next to her and she was relaxed.

After about an hour on the keyboard, she was reading what she wrote, when she caught a glimpse of movement out of the corner of her eye, out the front window. She looked up and felt a chill. Van Gogh suddenly stood and started barking loudly. She ran to the drawer and took out the gun, just as someone knocked at the door. She held the gun behind her and went to peek out the hole in the door. There was a man in a cable company uniform standing there.

She opened the door with the chain on, and asked what he wanted through the screen door. He smiled and said, "I'm upgrading the service out here, to increase the Internet speed. I'm sure you'd like faster Internet wouldn't you?"

"Let me see your ID badge?" she demanded.

58

He pulled his badge and held it up to the screen. She looked at it through the crack in the door, it looked legitimate, but ID badges could be faked. "Give me your office number so I can call to verify the badge."

He hesitated, then gave her a number. She tucked the gun in her belt and pulled her cell phone, dialing the number. It did go to the cable company, she waited, then asked the person who answered if there was a service person sent to upgrade her Internet. The person checked and said there was a request for upgrade, so the man was a representative of the company. She clicked off.

"Do you have to come in?" she asked.

"Just to check your wiring. Then I have to go up the pole to add an adapter to increase the speed of your connection," he said cheerfully.

Van Gogh was next to her growling quietly. She bent down, grabbed his collar and held him as she unhooked the chain and opened the door. The man opened the screen door, gave a look to the dog and smiled. "I hope you have a good hold on him?"

"I'll hold him until you are finished, then he'll go free. So don't take all day, I have work to do."

"No problem ma'am. I'll be quick. Now where is your computer?"

She pointed to the living room and he went that way. On the way there, he was looking around and then went to the computer. He looked at the connection and the

Fatal Departure

modem, then asked if there was cable in any other room. She pointed to the bed room and he went there and checked the connections to the TV. He left the room and said, "That's all, I'm done in here. I'll just check your wires attached to the house and go up the pole to improve your Internet. Thank you." He smiled and went out. Sarah let Van Gogh loose and put the gun back in the drawer.

She went to the desk and sat. She looked to the phone and thought about calling Dave. No, she said to herself, no sense worrying him. She looked out the window and saw the cable van moving away. Okay, she worried for nothing.

The van drove down the road along the front of the cemetery, then pulled in. The cable man pulled into a secluded area and parked. He went to the back of the van and opened the doors. He pulled out the naked body of the real service man, now in a plastic bag and dumped him behind a tombstone. He returned to the back of the now bloodied interior of the van and put the head in another bag. He was proud of his little deception.

He drove out the 101, about ten miles south, to where he left his car and pulled the truck up next to it. He got out, removed the uniform, wiped the truck clean of prints and set the truck to drive into the bushes off the side of the road. The truck drove forward until it hit a tree well into the brush, hiding it. He went to his car and drove away.

~~*~~

Dave was relaxing at his desk when Virgil came in. He sat at his desk and looked glum.

"What's the matter Virg?" Dave asked.

"I'm not good with dead bodies. Man, this job was so nice until this killer came to town. Do I have to see any more bodies?"

"Part of the job, buddy. I'm afraid there may be more."

"Oh man, I need to watch a few slasher movies on video to harden up. Can't you send Mike out on these murders?"

Mike perked up and said, "Like hell. You love driving the new cruiser so much, you can take the calls. I'll file papers and take complaints from old ladies wanting their neighbors arrested, but no murders. I didn't sign up for that."

"Mike, Virg, we are cops and have to take whatever we get, including being shot at. Now that's something worse than seeing a dead body. Okay?"

They both were silent, then Mike said under his breath, "Wussy."

"Hey I'm not a wussy, you pansy." Virgil shouted back.

"If the two of you don't stop, I'm sending you both on morgue detail to find out who the bodies are."

They both sat and went quiet, "Better," Dave said.

Fatal Departure

The phone rang and Dave picked it up since both men were still pouting. "Hello, Sheriff Chandler, may I help you?"

"Sheriff, this is Morgan from Hood Canal Communications. We sent a service van out on a request for service out your way and our vehicle tracking system said the thing was in an accident on Highway 101, about ten miles south of town. Can you investigate?"

"Do you have GPS on the vans?" Dave asked.

"Yes, we do. Do you have tracking?"

"Give me the codes and I'll investigate."

The person on the phone gave him the numbers, Dave thanked him and hung up, then Dave said to Virgil, "Let's test the new tracking system in the cruiser." They went out to the car and Virgil drove while Dave fiddled with the tracker.

They got to the area where the van was showing on the tracker, and stopped. They hunted through the bushes until they found the van stopped by a tree. Dave checked up front and saw no one, then pulled open the back doors of the truck and saw all the blood. Virgil went pale as Dave said, "This is getting worse."

*

Chapter 9

Dave and Virgil stood on the side of the road watching the State Police and their forensic team going over the van. The lead Detective came over and said, "Dave, are you opening your borders to serial killers now?"

"Don't even start that. I had enough with the killers that tried to take out my girlfriend. You were on that case too, as I remember."

"Yep, I was hoping to try and take the credit for bringing down the Slasher, but the report said you did it. So I had to bow to you. Now, what's your take on this?"

"Damned if I know. I have a friend in the FBI who is coming out, he thinks this may be related to a bunch of murders up in Seattle a couple years back. That case ended up with a detective being murdered, and they never caught the killer."

"So, the Feebies think this is the same guy?"

"Same M.O. as theirs, but this could be a totally different person. Haven't had any word from the killer as to what he's up to. Usually they leave little notes to taunt the police."

"You think you'll find the body of the cable guy?"

"I'm certain we'll find a black plastic bag around somewhere."

Fatal Departure

"Give me a call if you do find it. So we can tie it to the van. Have you called the cable company?"

"I told them they could have the van back after it's been processed."

"Good, I have a tow coming to take it into our lab for a thorough exam."

Someone called for the Detective and he excused himself from Dave. Virgil asked, "Where do you think the body is this time?"

"Virg, this is a big county and it could be anywhere. We'll just have to wait to hear from someone who stumbles across it. Let's go back to the office." Dave yelled to the detective that they were leaving and he waved him off.

"I'm dropping you off at the office and going home to check on Sarah. Don't start a fight with Mike now, you hear?"

"I have no problem with him, I'll be good." Virgil said with a sly smile.

Dave dropped him off and drove to the house. He pulled in and saw Sarah out back with the dog. She went in when she saw Dave pull up. He parked and went into the kitchen. Sarah was getting some coffee to give to Dave.

"Hey babe, all quiet here?" He took the cup and gave her a kiss.

"Yep, I've been working on my story. Any new bodies found?" she said as she was getting a glass for water from the cupboard.

He paused, but knew she'd find out sooner or later. "Not a body, but we found a cable company van with blood all over inside the back."

Dave was startled when he heard the drinking glass hit the floor and break. He looked to Sarah, her face was stricken with panic. "What! A cable van?" she sputtered the words.

"Yeah, what's the matter?" He went to her, carefully pulling her away from the broken glass.

"Oh my God! The cable guy was here. He was in the house!"

"What? When?"

"About two hours ago. He came by saying he had to install something to improve the Internet. I checked his ID and even called the company. It all seemed legitimate."

"What did he do? Why was he in the house?"

"He said he had to check our cable connections. He looked at the computer and the TV in the bedroom, then he went out to the pole."

"What pole?"

Fatal Departure

"I guess the one where the cables come from. I didn't see him, the poles are in the back. He left after about ten minutes of being out there. I saw him drive off."

"Could you remember his face?"

"He had on a hat that said Hood Canal Communications and he had a full, bushy beard with mustache. I didn't pay any attention to his eyes, but he had a big nose. I don't think I could give your sketch artist a good description."

"We don't have a sketch artist, but I'll have Warren Stevens, my FBI friend, take down what you saw. It sounds like he was disguised anyway, so may not do much good. Where was Van Gogh during all this?"

"I was holding his collar while the man was in the house. Van Gogh didn't care much for him," she said looking to the dog.

"Well, Van Gogh is an Airedale, the biggest of the terrier breed and they can be fearless, as he proved when he went after Harcourt as he tried to attack you. The British police use them for police dogs. I didn't worry about you too much with him around. Did the man seem frightened by Van Gogh?"

"Actually, he seemed worried at first, but I was holding Van Gogh back."

"Maybe it was good you had him in the house. So this guy must have wanted to see inside the house? I'm concerned now."

"So what should we do? I can carry your gun around with me, but I'd probably shoot you coming in the house."

"I believe you would. We need to get you to somewhere else." Dave said, thinking. "Maybe you could stay with Lois?"

"Oh no, not that. I like the woman, but she would drive me crazy."

"I know, we can go back to the Hood Canal house. You still own it and Lois can't sell it, so we could stay there."

Sarah thought on it, "If the killer could find this house, maybe he could find that house, too." She thought for a minute, then said, "Actually I like that idea, it gets me away from that cemetery. It creeps me out. Besides I know about the house alarms now and we could turn on the door alarms too."

"Works for me, if this guy was the killer, he wasted a day checking out this house." Dave said, glad that she wanted to move back to the big house. "Let's see how much stuff we can put in the Bronco and your car and start moving."

She went off to the bedrooms to get her suitcase and Dave went to the shed in the back and brought out some of the boxes they used to move here. They spent the next hour putting things in the cars and then Dave called his office.

After Mike answered, "Anything new going on there?" Dave asked.

Fatal Departure

"No, it's nice and quiet. Virgil and I are just playing Battleship and I'm whipping his ass."

"I'm glad you two have police duties to perform, are all the filing and reports done?"

"Yes, sir. All done and put away, and no complaints from any loonies so far."

"Okay, if you need me, call my cell phone. I'll be out of the house for a while."

"Roger that, I don't think we'll be bothering you any more tonight." Mike said and they finished the call.

"I hope not," Dave said after he clicked off the phone.

They had everything they would need for the night and drove out.

The drive down was pleasant, not much traffic on the highway. Dave was following Sarah as they reached the drive into the property. The house was just as they left it. Sarah went to the front door followed by Van Gogh and Dave. She still had spare keys and opened the door.

"Shall I carry you across the threshold?" Dave joked.

"No, but you can carry everything else in." She went to the living room, all the furniture was still there, so prospective buyers could see what it looked like furnished. She stood looking at the spot where Harcourt and Draegon were killed. It gave her a slight chill, but the place looked good after the crime scene cleaners did their magic.

Van Gogh went straight to the back door and stood looking out to the yard. Sarah went over and opened the door for the dog to go out and reminisce about his exploits with the animals. Hopefully no squirrels would be chasing him. She looked out to the waters of the Hood Canal and smiled. She loved the view and it was a thousand times better than the cemetery.

She studied the floor to ceiling window that replaced the one broken by the Slasher, Max Draegon. The window that saved her life, by sending an alarm signal to the police station. She smiled remembering how Dave rushed in, and snatched her from the jaws of death. Okay, that's overstating it, she thought, but that's how she felt.

Dave came in with a number of boxes, then Sarah went out to help. They had both cars unpacked within an hour and were setting up the kitchen. Sarah pulled out the steaks they brought and found the broiling pan. She put the meat in the oven and started dinner. Dave was in the living room, setting up Sarah's laptop and hooking it back up to the cable. Luckily they hadn't canceled it yet.

They ate the dinner and after the plates were washed, they were relaxing on the couch watching a show about alien visits. Sarah always enjoyed programs about visitors from outer space, it was something she firmly believed in. Dave pulled the curtains shut as it started to get dark, he wasn't taking any chances with prying eyes. He went to the control panel for the alarms and set the doors to respond to any opening. He tested the alarm warning in the house, causing Van Gogh to jump up and howl at the loud sound.

Sarah called to the dog and he jumped up on the couch with her. "Such a big brave dog, aren't you?" Dave came back and sat with Van Gogh between them, just as his cell phone rang.

"Crap, what now?" he said seeing the caller ID was Mike. He pushed the button to talk, "This better be good," he said into the phone. He listened then hung up. He put his head back on the couch and sighed loudly.

"Now what?" Sarah asked.

"They found the cable guy, in the cemetery, in a black plastic bag."

*

Chapter 10

"Who found him?" Dave asked Virgil, as he came up to the grave site. It was dark out now, but the lights on cemetery street poles illuminated the scene.

"Some woman on her way to put flowers on her late husband's grave. She saw the bag, but wouldn't have thought much about it, if she hadn't seen the blood dripping out of it," Virgil replied.

"Yep, not something you want to see coming from a big plastic bag. I'm surprised with this being such a small community, that people would know by now, if they saw a big plastic bag, there'd be a body in it."

"She came in from out of town. Her husband is from here, but she isn't."

"Ah, I see. So is the M.E. and his people getting pissed that we are giving them all this work to do?" Dave said with a frown.

"Well, Doc Norris is happy, he has all these bodies to work on, or so he says. He's been busy trying to get to the identities of the earlier bodies. We just figured this was the cable guy. But won't really know until they cross-match his blood. We just assumed it is."

"Never assume, Virg, it makes an ass out of you and me." Dave said, quoting the old saying.

Virgil thought a moment then said, "Oh, I get it now, ass, you, me. Assume."

"Very good Virg. Now we have to worry about how many more bodies are going to turn up."

"You can figure about a dozen more." Came a voice from behind them. Dave turned to look back and saw it was his friend, FBI Agent Warren Stevens.

"When did you get in town?" Dave asked as they shook hands.

"About an hour ago, some deputy in your office told me where to find you." He turned to another man behind him, "Dave, this is Special Agent Walt Meyers, one of those profilers you hear about."

71

Fatal Departure

Dave smiled and shook the man's hand and said, "And this is my deputy, Virgil Whitefield." They all shook hands.

"Dave, it's becoming more apparent that this is the same killer that stalked Seattle. His means of operation is too similar, from what your deputy told me at your office."

"Well, Mike has all the info so far. But there is one new development, the killer was in my house earlier. He pretended to be this cable guy and got Sarah to let him in to check the cable - just to get in our home."

"You're serious? He actually revealed himself to her?"

"Well, from What Sarah said, I think he was disguised. She says she couldn't really identify him."

"Interesting, we never had any reports that he revealed himself in Seattle. But then he may have and no one knew about it. He may be getting sloppy."

"Or in a rush to finish his quest," said Walt the profiler. Everyone turned to the smallish man. "Most serial killers will avoid contact unless they deem it necessary to further their goal. He is anticipating and possibly speeding up the reason for his kills and is moving in for the big goal."

"Kind of like Harcourt did with Sarah. He came across the country murdering people on his way to Sarah." Dave said.

Bob Moats

"Well, whatever he's doing, you have the full attention of the bureau at your disposal to catch him." Warren said.

"If all those people come in attacking, he may run. Wouldn't you say?" Dave asked.

"We can be subtle." Warren smiled.

"In a town of 1,200 people, even ten more people would be noticed." Dave said with a grin.

"This guy is not from here, we need to weed out the strangers and make him do something foolish."

"Like murder more people?" Virgil piped in.

Walt spoke again, "Other than the cable service man, he's bringing in bodies from out of the county, most likely Seattle. I've talked to the coroner earlier and he says the first couple bodies were of homeless people, they had the signs of living on the streets. Not having a normal life with a home and family. So he would be traveling back and forth, but he would have a base of operations here, to do his deeds of vivisecting the bodies. The cable man was a matter of convenience, handy and local. He probably arranged for a service call to your house and hijacked the van before the man could get there."

"So he needs a building to cut up the bodies. I think we can do a search on all rental businesses, or homes. Maybe we can locate him that way." Dave offered.

"Check with the local stores and see who's buying big garbage bags," Warren said with a grin.

73

Fatal Departure

"Warren, I'm sure he's bringing his equipment with him from Seattle. I'm sure he's not dumb enough to buy them here." Dave said. "Where are you staying?"

"Haven't found a place yet, know of a good motel?"

"Hold on," he said and pulled his cell phone. He dialed a number and waited. "Hey babe, I got you protection."

An hour later, Dave, Warren and Walt were in Sarah's home, Dave having cleared it with her.

"Warren, meet Sarah Keller, bravest woman I know." Dave smiled.

"Good to finally meet you, I've read the files on your incident, you were brave."

"Thank you, but it was Dave who came to my rescue."

"That's Dave, always the hero." Warren said, and then introduced Walt. "So where do we sleep, on the couch?

"No, there is a second bedroom, but no bed, so you will have to sleep on the floor." Dave said.

"Oh no, we have that covered." The black van that they drove out in had plenty of equipment for stakeouts, including cots. They brought in all that they needed to sleep for the night and set up in the bedroom.

They all went out to the living room and relaxed, Dave passed out beers, then they sat talking about the murders.

"So the FBI has no idea why the detective was murdered, no last word on it?" Dave asked.

"No," said Walt, "There was no word left for the reason, or none that could be found. We investigated his connections to many of his prior cases, none rang any alarms."

"Let me throw this out to you, did the detective have any connection with The NY Slasher?"

"I'm not sure, I'll put some people on it. But isn't the Slasher dead?"

"He is, but make me happy by checking." Dave said.

"It will be done." Walt said efficiently and then went out of the room pulling his cell phone.

"He's a good kid, I like him," said Warren.

"I thought you wanted to be a profiler too?" Dave asked Warren.

"They say it takes a PhD in psych and a whole lot of other degrees. I have no patient for school. I'm happy where I'm at, I get to shoot people." He grinned and then Dave asked if he wanted another beer.

"Does the sun rise in the East?" he laughed.

Fatal Departure

About two hours later, after they caught up on old memories, they went to bed. Dave and Sarah went off to the bedroom and got ready to crash.

"I don't have much to do tomorrow, can I come in to the station and help Mike play Battleship." She giggled.

"You know that would be a good idea, now that you mention it. You could come in everyday and work with us, Mike would teach you the system and then he wouldn't be stuck in the desk job. So you okay with this?"

"Sure, I need to get away from my book for a while. I could help."

"Tomorrow is Saturday, so I normally don't go in, but I think with this trouble I need to get more time on the job. We can keep busy investigating. And now that the FBI is here, we can't just take days off."

"Agreed, we go to work and bring this bastard to justice." Sarah said with a flourish of her hand.

Dave kissed her and said, "Tonight, I'm going to bring you to justice."

"Oh, can we use the handcuffs?" she smiled.

Early the next morning, Sarah had fixed everyone pancakes and everyone said they tasted great. She was pleased. They all got ready to leave and arrived at the station to find Mike and Virgil talking to six people at the counter. They were having a loud discussion and when Dave came in, the people went straight to him, yelling all at once. Warren was ready to pull his handgun, but Dave laughed and told him to hold.

"Okay people, now one at a time, Harry you speak first," he said to an elder man.

The man stood in front of the small mob and said, "What are you doing to stop these killings in our town?"

"Well, Harry and all you others, the only person who was murdered localiy was a cable man, and he was from Tacoma. The rest of the bodies are from homeless people out of Seattle. So far, no one here has been murdered. This killer has an agenda and it doesn't seem to include you guys. Now go home or to work and relax. If anyone gets murdered here, call me. Virgil, will you escort these fine people out?"

He came around the counter and politely said, "If you will follow me, please." They all went out.

"I'd say the average age of that group is about eighty?" Warren kidded.

"Yes, they are. It's an old community, but a lot of young people are settling here now. We lose older people and gain younger ones. It's a constant flux of people. But the killer is not helping the publicity for living here."

"And the killer is adding bodies to your population." Walt said.

*

Chapter 11

Dave introduced Mike to everyone and said, "Mike, I want you to teach Sarah everything about the office, including dispatch on the radio. She's going to help for a few days until we catch the bastard killing people." He turned to Sarah and said, "You are now a student and there will be a quiz. So learn well, grasshopper."

She smiled and Mike told her to come around the counter and he'd start. She went there with Van Gogh in tow, tying him to the pipe of a radiator on a nearby wall. He sat watching the people moving around.

"Where's your private office, Dave," Warren asked.

Dave laughed and pointed to a desk and smiled, saying, "That's it. I've thought about getting cubicle walls, but I like seeing what's going on. We do have a small room we use for conferences, we can set up in there." He led them to the room in the back. It was small, about ten by ten, with a small table and four chairs, but enough room for them to plot their attack.

Walt said, "I'll go get our file cases and bring them in." He left and then Dave turned to Warren.

"He's a little young, has he handled any big cases lately?"

"Walt is capable of handling the situation. Okay, he's a newbie, but he's sharp and has a photographic memory, almost eidetic. He annoys the hell out of me when I tell a story and he corrects me in front of women I'm trying to impress."

"Now that would be annoying for you." Dave said.

"Yep, but he can keep all the facts in his head and recall them when we need them. He's handy for reference. So what's your plan?'

"We have no plan; this is all happening too fast. I sat with Virgil and Mike yesterday and we couldn't come up with anything."

"Okay, we need to check out rental buildings for this creep to work out of. Then we need to contact the cable company and find out how and when the call for service came in and where the service guy was supposed to go. The killer had to be the one who called, so he could grab the van and outfit to get into your house. Can you get a big map of the area, so we can put it on the wall and mark the spots he dumped bodies?"

"Sure, we have a topographical map, I'll get it." Dave left the room and Warren sat in a chair by the table and took out his cell phone. He called the FBI office back in Seattle and asked for an Agent Fielding.

"Doug, I need you to follow up on a call to Hood Canal Communications for a service request out here yesterday. I'll have Walt give you all the details, he knows them better than I do." He paused, listened and then said, "Thanks, talk later." He clicked off and waited for everyone to get back.

Fatal Departure

Walt came back in with two briefcases and set them on the table, then sat on a chair, quietly opening the cases and pulling out the contents. Warren asked him to contact Fielding about the cable company service call. He said he would. Dave entered with a map and a roll of tape.

The map was taped to the wall and they started to mark where the bodies were dumped and the location of the van. They stood back staring at it and then Dave asked, "What are we seeing?"

Warren paused, then said, "Not much, is there? Two dumps in the cemetery and one on the beach."

Dave spoke, "Something that's been bothering me, the killer dumped the first body in a grave hole, it seemed he was more hiding it than leaving it out for us to find. It didn't seem to be an attempt to taunt us."

Walt cleared his throat, "In the Seattle killings, the person dumped about 16 of the 20 bodies out where they could be found easily. We only found the other four by accident, mostly people discovering them. The bags were the same, but the dumps were not easily found. You can expect the killer to start dumping a body or more out in the open soon, on a highway or in front of a business. He steps up his kills and thrills that way."

Dave smiled at Walt's reference to kills and thrills. "He evidently didn't leave many clues to his identity back then?"

"No, he was careful to cover his tracks," Warren said.

Bob Moats

Dave thought back to what he had read about the NY Slasher, and how he left no clues either. And got away clean until he came to Brinnon. Dave smiled at how he was the only one to take out the Slasher.

"What are you smiling about?" Warren asked Dave.

"Just thinking about something, not important," he said, as Virgil came in.

"Boy, those seniors take forever getting in their cars." He looked to the map, went over, studied it and said, "Interesting, if you draw a line from the beach drop, through the two bodies in the cemetery, the line would continue on right through your property Dave."

Dave was sitting on the edge of the table and stood now, going to the map. "Wow, it does, but that has to be coincidence. Good eye, Virgil."

"As you said, it could be just coincidence, but it's something." Warren said. "Like he's pointing to your place."

"If we get more bodies and the line changes towards the Hood Canal house, I'm moving Sarah again." Dave frowned at the thought.

"If we keep her surrounded, you won't have to worry. Besides, he may be after you. Did you think of that?" Warren offered.

"Can you bring in a few agents to camp out in the old house he thinks we'll be in? Maybe he'll do something dumb and get caught." Dave asked.

81

Fatal Departure

Warren said, "It's a good idea, and the place will look lived in. Walt, call for reinforcements, but warn them to be discrete coming in." He turned to Dave, "We should put Sarah's car in the drive and leave the FBI unit cars here at the station. They can drive her car to the house."

"Works for me, I'll tell Sarah." He went out as Walt called. Warren and Virgil were studying the map.

"If we go by the imaginary line, what is between the beach and the cemetery?" Warren asked Virgil.

Virgil looked closer to where a line would go through, "There's the highway, a few homes, an auto repair shop and a bait shop. Think he might drop a body in with the bait?"

Warren laughed, "I hope not, but they're worth watching."

Dave came back a few minutes later and said Sarah was alright with the plan. Walt came back in and said, "There will be three agents coming from Seattle and they'll be ready to stake out inside the house."

"Good, now we need to find his base of operations here. Dave, can you find out where there are rental buildings?"

"I can talk to Lois Carter, local real estate agent, she may know. We can check with the newspaper out of Seattle, the Sun Times classifieds to see if they had any listings."

"Walt, call Fielding back in the office and have him go through the recent paper classifieds to see if there is any listings for rental places in Brinnon," Warren said, and the man went back out of the room to call.

"I think you like having Walt for the grunt work, don't you," Dave said quietly to Warren.

"I'm keeping him busy." He winked and grinned.

A hour later, Dave called Lois in and they were talking to her. She only knew of two rentals available and they were both still empty. "Virgil, take those addresses from Lois and go check the places. Take Mike in case you find the killer, just be careful."

Virgil acknowledged and went out. Dave followed him and asked Sarah if she was good watching the office alone.

"I think I can handle it, not really much to do and with Mike's instructions, I figured out the radio so I can call for the cavalry. How's it going in there?" she said.

"Well, we are progressing a little. I'm just hoping the killer slips up and we can end this."

Lois came out of the room and stood at the counter. "I have a showing on the house later today, I'm hoping they will buy."

Dave cleared his throat and said, "Uh, Lois, that's a problem. Now, this is not to be told to anyone at all, and I mean it. Sarah and I are back in the house, the killer knows the location of the one we were in and we needed to go somewhere he may not know about. It will only be until we catch the person, so cancel all showings until I tell you. Please," he added.

"I see, a hideout. No problem, I'll call the people and cancel. I'll make some excuse. I hope you find this person, everyone in town is on pins and needles about the killings," she said.

"Well, as I said to a concerned group earlier, the killings have all been of people from out of the area. But that doesn't mean it won't happen here, so let them know to be cautious of strangers. Hey, since you seem to know everyone, call me if you see any strange people loitering in town."

"I'll do that and I'll put a few of my gossipy friends on the alert too," she beamed and said good-bye, then left.

"I may regret asking her to do that," Dave said to Sarah, "She'll be calling me now for every tourist in town. I'll let her know to call you and you can take the info."

"Well thank you, I love you too."

*

Chapter 12

Dave looked a little surprised. "I know you were just kidding, but you've never actually said you love me. I can be patient until you feel comfortable to actually say it, and mean it."

Sarah came around the counter, put her arms around his neck and whispered in his ear. "I love you, and will forever." Then she kissed him.

Warren came out of the room, "Eeyuw, mushy stuff. Get a grip or a room. We have a killer to catch."

"Shut up Warren, you're just jealous you don't have a hot babe like I do." Dave said with another kiss to Sarah.

"Agreed, now can you come up for air. I got a call from Fielding in Seattle and he contacted Hood Canal Communications. I had Walt talk to him to get all the details. Walt, tell the Sheriff what Doug told you."

Walt came forward and said, "The cable company took a call yesterday at 9:35 am, and the caller said that their cable was down, from the storm, and they were without cable TV or Internet. The caller insisted that they come out at a certain time so someone would be there. The address they gave was 2134 Church Road. Is that the address of your house?"

Dave looked concerned, "Yes it is. The killer had to have known the address before he called. Did they say if he gave a name?"

"Of course, the cable representative asked, and was told Davis Chandler." Walt answered.

"He knows my formal name, he's got to be after me. That had to be the reason he's using my name and home to have lured the service man out. Do they have any voice recording of the call?"

"They do, it's procedure for them to record all customer services calls for quality and training. Doug Fielding is getting a subpoena for the recording, then they will have it analyzed. We don't have any recordings of the Seattle killer, so we can't cross-check it, but if any more calls come in, we will be able to."

"Dave, you had to have pissed this guy off somewhere, probably in Tacoma when you were on the PD there? Can you get the case files from them that you were on, that may have led him to this hate?"

"I can call a friend and see if he can send the files, or at least look through them. I didn't pull too many crime cases, mostly small things like disturbances and break-ins. I'll call him later."

The radio crackled and a voice came over it, Sarah went to it and pushed the right button. Into the microphone she said, "Come in."

"Say over," Dave told her.

"Over."

"This is Virgil and we checked both places, they are deserted. No sign of activity, over."

Dave said to tell them to come back, Sarah repeated that and said, "Over and out."

"Very good," Dave said with a smile. "I just may hire you permanently."

"We'll see about that," Sarah said and sat at Virgil's desk.

The phone on Virgil's desk rang, startling Sarah. She answered. "Hello, Sheriff's office." She listened and wrote something on the pad of paper on the desk. She said someone would be there shortly and hung up. She tore the paper off the pad and handed it to Dave.

He looked at it, turned to the men and said, "A body was dumped at Ernie's Bait Shop."

Warren smiled and said, "Virgil will love this."

They were at the bait shop about twenty minutes later, after Dave had Sarah call and tell Mike and Virgil to go there. He told her to call the M.E.'s office and inform them of the body. They arrived and found Virgil and Mike already there.

"This is not good for my business, Sheriff!" The man identified as Ernie shouted. "I sell bait and tackle, not bodies!"

"Okay Ernie, take it easy. The coroner will be here shortly to take the body away. Meanwhile all your customers will have to wait." He looked around at the deserted store. "Now tell me what happened."

"As you know, I live in the back and I closed for lunch and when I came back out from my room, I opened the front door and found the black bag on the steps. I knew right away what it was from the rumors going around. The guy had to have drove up and dumped the body, then took off."

"You didn't move the bag at all?"

"No sir, I left it where it was. I didn't touch it either. I don't touch dead bodies, only dead fish."

Warren smiled to Virgil and said, "Well, you called it right for the bait shop. Have you thought about a future with the FBI?"

"Nope, I'd actually have to work then." He said and went out to greet the coroner's people driving up.

Doc Norris led his people to the bag and he knelt down to it. He took a knife and cut the bag, then called for Dave.

"What do you need Doc?" Dave asked.

"I thought you said you had a body?"

"Yeah. It's the same as the others. Right?"

"Nope, this one is a pig, of the pork variety. Looks like a fresh kill too. But definitely not a body. Same bag though, same as the killer's other bags. He's screwing with you now." He stood and told his people to go back to the morgue.

Warren was looking to the carcass and said, "I think this is a statement. Pig."

Mike said, "If it's a fresh kill as Doc said, maybe we could have a pig roast."

Everyone stared at him until he was uncomfortable. "What?" he finally said.

"Mike, you are now officially the animal control officer. Take the pig back to the office and put him in…" he stopped to think, then looked to Warren, "Is this thing part of a real crime scene?"

"Well, not really, if you had an ASPCA you could file a complaint. But we don't have a crime, unless littering is a crime here?"

"Fine, this is really sucking. Mike, take it to Harold's butcher shop and have him put it in his cold room, until we can decide what to do with it. Virgil, help him." The two men struggled with the bag and took it to the patrol car, putting it in the trunk. They drove off.

Dave turned to Ernie, "Well, you didn't have a body, if that's any consequence. We'll get out of your way, so the customers can flock in now. Thanks."

Dave, Warren and Walt left the building and stood by the cars in the parking lot. "This was just a way of saying screw you cop. A pig? It's definitely aimed at me," Dave said.

"It at least wasn't a human. Now we need to find out where he got the pig. Any farms around here?" Warren asked.

Fatal Departure

"A couple out of town. We can hit both of them in less than an hour, shall we go?"

"Lead the way pig boy." Warren laughed as Dave took a swat at him, missing.

They went to the first farm and the man there said he had all his pigs, then they drove over to the second. "Sure, I had a pig come up missing, some bastard in a van took him from my pigpen and drove away." He was irate and pissed.

"You saw the man take the pig?" Warren asked.

"Hell no, I came out of the house just as he as driving away from the pen. I checked the pen, and one of the five pigs was missing."

"Well Amos, we have the pig, but unfortunately it's dead." Dave said to the man.

"Damn, I was going to let it get a little bigger before butchering it. Where's it at?"

"We took it to Harold's butcher shop. I'll call and tell him you're coming to get it."

"Let me call, I usually have Harold take care of the butchering anyway."

"Good, now can you identify the van?"

"Yeah, it was small Ford, all white and had no markings. I didn't get the plates, it was too far away."

"Okay Amos, thanks." He walked away with Warren and Walt in tow. They got into the patrol car and drove out.

Dave got on his cell phone and called Virgil, "Virg, be on the lookout for an all-white Ford van, check whatever you can find, but be cautious if it's some tourist, we don't want any harassment complaints. The stolen pig was in the van, and it had to have been killed in it. Call if you find the van." He hung up and looked to Warren, "What now super-agent?"

"Honestly, all we can do is follow the leads and hope he screws up. We got zip for now."

They drove back to the office and went in. Sarah was playing with Van Gogh and then stood when they came in.

"Hi, did you find the pig farm?" she asked.

"Yes, it was Amos Peart's farm, but all is good with him. Been quiet here, I presume?"

"Yep, all's well on the home front, and I have the shotgun under the counter to handle the unruly people. So you can relax."

"Good, we'll be in the room trying to figure out what we're doing." He leaned over the counter and kissed her. They all went to the back and Sarah went back to playing with Van Gogh.

About a block down from the Sheriff's office, the Toyota Corolla sat with the man behind the wheel. He was watching the activities of the police and grinning about his pig stunt. Time to really lay on the murders. Maybe someone the Sheriff knows personally this time.

*

Chapter 13

There were no more reports of any dumpings and it was getting late, so Dave put Virgil in charge of the office for the night and told Mike to relieve him around four in the morning. Dave was wishing he had a bigger police force, just to cover all the shifts.

Warren said, "You and Sarah drive home in your Bronco, and then Walt and I will follow a ways behind, to see if you're being tailed."

"Good idea, I'll take the long scenic route to get there. Most of those roads are long stretches and easy to spot someone following." He turned to Sarah, "Shall we take our baby home?"

Sarah attached Van Gogh's leash to his collar and they went out to Dave's car. The ride home took a good half hour for a normal ten minute trip. Warren was satisfied that no one followed them.

As they pulled into the Hood Canal house drive, Warren's cell buzzed. He answered and it was the leader of the team of men who were going to stake out the other house. He handed off the phone to let Walt explain how to get to where they were, so they could change cars before going to the house.

Everyone exited their cars and Warren told Dave that the men were in the area.

"Good, when they get here, they can take Sarah's car and go to the house. I'll get the extra keys for the house." He went in and rummaged through a box, removing the keys and handing them to his friend.

Sarah went to the kitchen and looked into the refrigerator, found nothing that would feed everyone. She told Dave and he said, "Warren and I can lead the agents to the house and on the way back, we'll stop and get some fast food. We didn't even think to eat today, did we?"

"I had a candy bar that was in my purse. You guys were so busy I didn't want to interrupt your work with mention of food," she said.

"When the agents get here, I'm taking Warren and we'll lead them to the house, then we'll stop to get some food," he told her again.

"No donuts, please."

He smiled and kissed her. There was a noise from out front and everyone took their weapons out. It was the team of agents coming onto the porch. After introductions were made, Dave organized the plan and they all went to their cars and took off leaving Sarah and Walt in the house.

Fatal Departure

"How long have you been a Special Agent, Walt?" Sarah asked the young man sitting on the couch looking uncomfortable.

"I've been with the bureau for about two years, mostly in the intelligence sector, but I've been a field agent for about six months. This is a little intimidating with all these murders, I mean seeing all the bodies. I've heard about the serial killings around the country and in Seattle but never got to go out to see a crime scene. Before we came here yesterday, we stopped at the morgue to talk to the coroner about the bodies they had. It wasn't pleasant seeing the corpses."

"So this is your first case of a serial killer?"

"Yes," he said simply.

"And all the blood and gore didn't bother you?"

"It does, if you let it. I've conditioned my mind to not let it affect me."

"I wish I could do that," Sarah said quietly.

"You had a traumatic experience with the serial killers in this house, it's hard to let go of the pain and memory."

"Yes, it is," she said looking to the spot where the killers were sent to hell, remembering all the blood on the floor. The cleaners did a great job, but had to replace the carpets. It looked almost like a whole new room now.

"Well, I just have to harden up, and get over it," she said. "Would you like some coffee?"

"Do you have any soda?"

"We did bring some with us, I'll get you one." She left the room and went to the refrigerator. She came back and turned on the TV after handing the can to Walt. They sat quietly watching the television.

~~*~~

Dave led the agents to the house and pulled into the drive. Dave got out and looked around the area, just to be sure there was no one watching. It was now slightly dark out, so they could get in hopefully unnoticed.

"Okay, guys," Dave said to the three agents inside the house, "Make yourself at home, just stay out of my wife's closet. She doesn't like men wearing her dresses. I know, I've tried, and she got quite mad." They laughed and he continued, "There still should be a little food in the kitchen, plenty of can goods, so use them. You can watch the cemetery across the road, a couple bodies were dumped there. There's cable TV and Internet if you have your laptops." He handed his business card to the lead agent and said, "Call immediately if anything develops. Don't wait, this man is very dangerous, so don't take chances."

"We'll be cautious, sir. Thanks." The agent said, and they went to get their equipment from the car.

Dave and Warren said they were leaving, got into the Bronco and drove away.

Fatal Departure

"So how's married life," Warren joked, as they drove to get food.

"I love the woman, and I plan on keeping her, even if we don't get married. It will be her decision, when she's ready. She still has some feelings for her late husband, and I have to be cautious not to be pushy."

"That was the husband who was murder by Harcourt?"

"Yes, so it was never a complete break like in a divorce. I know she hurts, her first bad dream involved the bedroom where she found her husband and her best friend murdered. Harcourt tried to make it look like they were having an affair that went to murder-suicide, but the forensics said the killings were done by another person. It was very hard on her. Then to meet the man who committed the murders, not good."

"You said earlier today that she's going to see a shrink? Think it will help?"

"I'm hoping it will, but I just have to be there for her. Well, what do we have here," Dave said noticing a white van parked off the side of the highway. He pulled over next to the van and they got out, drawing their weapons. They carefully went to the van and looked in. Warren pulled the back doors open, as Dave held his gun out. There was no one in the van, but they found a good amount of blood on the floor of the back.

"We found our pig thief get-away vehicle," he said as he pulled his cell phone to call Virgil.

"Wait. There's not much that can be done tonight, it's late and the van isn't going anywhere. Wait till morning, we can disable the engine so the killer can't come back and use it." Warren said as Dave put his cell phone back in his pocket. They popped the hood, reached in and removed the distributor cap and pulled a few wires. They closed the van back up and got back in their cars.

"I'll call Virgil to call State Police forensics to come in and get the van in the morning."

They drove on as Dave watched the rear view mirror for anyone following. Then they stopped at the Halfway House, got burgers and fries for take-out. The food arrived and they left.

They got to the house and went in setting off the alarms. Van Gogh went crazy and nearly attacked Warren coming in. Sarah managed to grab him and Dave shut down the alarm, calling Virgil to ignore the signal in the office.

"Being extra careful Sarah?" Dave asked.

"Of course, I'm not giving the killer any chance to get at us."

"Works for me," he said as he turned on the alarms again. They all went to the living room and Warren handed out the food. They sat eating and watching TV. No one was talking about the murders, they needed some mental relief.

Fatal Departure

The next morning they got ready to go to the station. They went out and Warren followed Dave in their van. Mike was standing outside the office talking to a man. Dave parked and went to them.

"Morning Mike. What's going on?" Dave asked, as everyone came up behind him.

"Dave, this is Mr. Greg Harding. He drove here from Tacoma and was asking about his rental property. He was over to the building and the locks were changed. The man he rented it to hasn't responded to his calls about the rent. Seems the renter's check bounced."

Dave and Warren both perked up at the mention of a rental building.

"Mr. Harding, come in and we'll see if we can help." They all went in and Dave led the man to the conference room, asking him to sit.

"Mr. Harding, who is the man renting your building?"

"He called me about my ad in the Seattle Sun Times and we met at a Starbuck in town. He gave me a check and I forgot to deposit it until a few days ago. The bank called and said it bounced. It's not the first time I've had a rubber check from a tenant. I came down to talk to Mr. Webber, that was his name, and I found the building all closed up and the locks changed. I have the right to enter the building, it's in the lease. Now I need you to do something about it. I didn't want to break in, that's not the way I do business. I do it legally."

"Okay, Mr. Harding, we'll follow you out and check on the building. Mike, you and Sarah hold down the fort."

Dave, Warren and Walt followed the man out to the cars and they drove out to a building in the woods, west of town. Dave told Mr. Harding to wait by the cars as he and Warren went to the building, with their guns drawn.

Mr. Harding turned to Walt, still standing by him. "Is this how you treat check bouncers in your town?"

Walt actually laughed, breaking his usually somber expression. "You're from out of town. We have a serial killer loose and your building may be where he's hiding out."

"Are you shitting me? I need to check references better."

*

Chapter 14

Warren peeked into a window, but it was covered with papers. "Can't see in, has to be the place." They went around to the door in front, Warren gave it a good kick and the door gave. They flew in holding their guns out, hoping for the killer to try and draw on them. The room was empty.

They stood surveying the room, there was a door on the side that was open and they could see a table with

Fatal Departure

plastic covering it. The plastic was covered in blood. Dave was hearing a sound, like a clock ticking. He looked around the room and then he saw over the door they came through, a box with wires going down to the door. The box had a red blinking light.

Dave grabbed Warren yelling, "Bomb," and pulled him out of the building. They managed to get to the cars just as the building blew with such force all the men were knocked off their feet. Luckily, no one was hurt.

"That son of a bitch booby trapped the building. Great." Warren was yelling trying to clear his ears from the ringing.

Mr. Harding stood staring at his building. "Shit, who is going to replace my building?" he moaned.

"Don't you have insurance?" asked Walt.

Harding thought, then said, "Yeah, they'll pay for this. I'll need a police report to give them."

Dave said, "I'll see you get one, now you need to describe the man, after we get back to the station."

The building was in flames; Dave called the Fire Department and gave them the information. About ten minutes later, the fire trucks arrived and they worked on quelling the blaze. Dave told the Fire Chief to give him a report on the building, and then he said it was caused by a bomb. The Chief said his investigators would contact him.

Dave rounded up everyone and went back to the office. Sarah was standing on the front stoop of the station watching the smoke in the distance. They pulled up and got out.

"We heard the blast all the way here," Sarah said after Dave filled her in. "I was worried that it had something to do with you."

"I'm safe, but my ears are still ringing," he smiled and they all went in and took Harding to the conference room.

"Now Mr. Harding, do you have the bounced check with you?" Warren asked.

"I do," he said and pulled it out. Warren took it by the edge and gave it to Walt, who pulled a plastic bag from his pocket and put the check in. "Have you ever been fingerprinted, Mr. Harding?"

"Yes, for the Army. Why?"

"So we can eliminate your prints on the check."

Dave asked, "Can you describe the man?"

"He was about average height, your height Sheriff, and a full beard, mustache and a rather large nose. He was dressed like an outdoor person, which he said was why he wanted to rent my building, to do some deer hunting."

"You didn't wonder about the fact that it's not deer season?"

"I don't know one season from another. I just buy buildings and rent them."

Fatal Departure

"Like a slum lord," Warren said.

"Please, don't be so crass, I'm fair with my rents."

"Okay, did he say anything about himself?"

"He said he was from Seattle but wanted a place over here for his hunting."

"How far in advance did he pay?" Dave asked.

"Two months, with option for six more, if he liked the building."

"Okay Mr. Harding, please leave your contact information with my deputy and we'll be in touch about the building. You can go now."

The man thanked them and left. Mike came in and said, "I called the forensic people about the van, they'll go out this morning and get it." He went back out.

"This is getting complicated. Murder, bodies, pigs slaughtered, now a bombed building. You sure know how to show a guy a good time," Warren joked.

"Anytime you feel overwhelmed, you can leave." Dave laughed.

"Walt, pack up and let's go home," Warren said to the agent. He started to leave and Warren said, "Hey, I was kidding. Relax." Walt stopped, looking confused.

"Walt, go out and get the check delivered back to Seattle," he turned to Dave, "You do have overnight delivery?"

"Yes, we do - USPS, the post office. They'll get it delivered. Walt, have Mike take you to the post office." Walt went out.

"You think they'll get any prints off the check?" Dave asked.

"Never can tell, every bit of evidence helps. Speaking of that, have forensics go over the bombed building to see what they can find." Warren asked.

"I'll call and let them know. I think we're going to use up all our relationship with the State Police people."

"It's their job and they need the work, things are slow lately. You've got the most excitement around the state."

I'll be glad to pass it off to anyone who wants it." Dave said with a laugh.

~~*~~

The man was watching the fire department working hard to be sure the fire was totally out, so not to start a forest fire. He was not happy, but glad his booby trap worked, destroying all evidence of him being there. Now he had to find another place to work on his crimes. He looked to his map and saw a road nearby, maybe there was a place somewhere there he could get into and set up. He drove out and saw a house sitting alone off the road. The drive was overrun with weeds, looking like they hadn't been tended to in a while. He sat watching the building, seeing no one moving, he drove in the drive up to the house.

He got out of his car and looked back to the road, it was well hidden by the brush growing wild. He hoped the house owners weren't someone who would be missed in town. He went to the door and knocked. About a couple minutes later and older woman answered.

"Yes, young man do you want something? If not, get off my property." The man could see this woman was not a very friendly person.

"May I speak with your husband?"

The woman just stared at him. "I have no husband, the bastard ran off with my best friend and no one was very sympathetic about it. Screw all those people. Now talk or get lost."

"Ma'am, you really should be nicer, you could have lived longer," he said, as he pulled the long knife from its holder. The woman screamed, but her scream went unnoticed.

He wrapped the body in a plastic bag, after he removed the head, on the woman's kitchen table, covered with a plastic table cloth. He had his next victim to drop for the Sheriff. But he didn't want to let them know who this woman was, or they'd be at his door again. Luckily, he was away from the last building when they showed up. Too bad they weren't killed in the explosion.

He took the body out to his car and placed it in the trunk. He stood looking at the bag and was thinking about a good place to dump it. He closed the trunk and took the map he had, out of the car. He was smart enough to keep all his personal things in the car, in case he had to get out of town quickly. He opened the map and studied the area. He saw what he was looking for, a perfect dumping place.

~~*~~

Dave was sitting at his desk with Sarah on the chair next to the desk. "You do know you have an appointment with Dr. Gladwin tomorrow?"

"Thanks for reminding me," Sarah said sarcastically. "What time again?"

"At one, I can take you or have Virgil drive, if I'm busy on the case."

"I can drive myself."

"You don't have your car, remember?"

"Oh. That's right. Okay, Virgil can drive me then."

"Fine with me, he won't mind getting away from crime."

Warren came out from the conference room and stood at the counter. "Walt just talked to Fielding and they got the voice recording from the cable company. Tells us nothing really. May I ask a question?"

Fatal Departure

"I suppose so if you really need to ask. Shoot." Dave replied.

"Why do you have such a small station?"

"We're actually a sub-station of the Jefferson County Sheriff's office, but we are autonomous. They let us run our own business out here."

"Why do you use the State Police then, why not the County Sheriff?"

"Just say that we get better response from the State Police and they're closer. Also political reasons, too numerous to talk about." Dave answered.

"Just like the Seattle Police doesn't like the Seattle FBI interfering in their cases."

"About the same." Dave smiled.

The phone rang and Dave reached for it, "Sheriff's office." He listened and then wrote something on a pad and hung up. "We got another body," he said frowning.

Warren called for Walt and Dave kissed Sarah, "We'll be back as soon as possible. Mike, take care of the place." The three men went out and to their cars.

Dave led in the new patrol car, he liked the power it had and the smooth ride. He was almost lost in thought about the car, when he remembered he was supposed to be going to a crime scene. To a place that he didn't want a crime scene to be at. Warren and Walt followed in their van, trying to keep up with Dave.

106

They arrived at the local elementary school and pulled up to the playground. Luckily, it was Sunday, so there were no children in the playground. They saw that the plastic bag was placed on one of the swings.

*

Chapter 15

The school janitor waved to them as they parked. They walked across the dusty ground to the swings and Dave said, "Howdy Jake. It's Sunday, why are you here?"

"I came in to wax the hall floors. I took a break to have a smoke and came out from the building. I looked over here and saw the bag. I knew what it was right away, so I called you guys."

"Good thing it's the weekend, or there would have been a few upset children." Warren pointed out.

"I'm sure most of the children don't know about the bag dumps. They probably would think it was just trash left by someone. I'll get Doc Norris, but I'm sure he won't like having his Sunday disturbed." Dave went to the patrol car and used the radio to call Mike.

About an hour later, the M.E. crew had the bag on the ground and cut open. Doctor Steve Davis filled in for Norris, who was out on the Hood Canal fishing. Davis was examining the headless body, then stood.

Fatal Departure

"It does look like a homeless person, as you said the others were. The body hasn't seen a bath in a long while and there are sores on the backside, probably from sleeping on the ground. That's my preliminary evaluation, but I'll know better when I do the full autopsy."

"Thanks Steve, make up your report and I'll pick it up." He turned to Warren, "This one is different though, it's a woman. The others were men."

"The Seattle killer did murder both men and women, so this follows the pattern," Walt added.

"Whatever! This is getting ridiculous. We need to find this bastard and stop him," Dave was mad now. "If this son-of-a-bitch wants me, then he should just come and get me, and stop this dumping crap."

"He is playing with you, just like the Seattle killer did with the detective he murdered. He won't reveal himself; he'll keep killing until he manages to get under your skin and then gets to you." Warren said.

"Maybe I should put myself out there, so he can get to me. I'd love to meet him."

"Let's see what we can do to stop him first before we use you for bait."

The body was removed from the playground and the area was ready for the children to in play happily tomorrow. They were back to the station and Sarah asked what happened. Dave told her, as he sat next to her.

"How are you going to stop him?" she asked.

"Hopefully he'll screw up and we get a bead on him. He's out there somewhere and we have no clue as to where." Dave said, now sounding frustrated.

Warren and Walt were standing at the counter, "Listen, not much we can do at the moment, I don't know about anyone else, but I'm hungry. If you guys want to eat, let's go. I'm not going another day without food, I'm skinny enough."

"Skinny yes, but your butt is huge, too much sitting around." Dave laughed.

"Well, I'm going to park my fat ass in the Halfway House and devour a big juicy burger and greasy fries. So, I'm out of here, follow if you dare." He looked to Walt, pointed to the door and they went out.

"Are you hungry?" Dave asked Sarah.

"Yes."

They went out after Dave told Mike to call if anything happens. Mike went over to a file cabinet and took out a paper bag. He sat and ate his lunch, enjoying the quiet of the room.

All was peaceful the rest of the afternoon, no calls from Seattle FBI or State Police forensics bringing good news. After they ate at the restaurant, they drove by the morgue. Dave asked Sarah if she wanted to wait in the car.

Fatal Departure

"Hell no, I'm strong enough to go in there." She said firmly.

Dave grinned and took her to the building, followed by Warren and Walt. They entered the building, went down the hallway to the autopsy room. The building was totally silent, being as it was Sunday. They could hear voices coming from the room as they entered.

"Steve," Dave called to the M.E., standing over the body on the table talking into a microphone, recording his exam of the body.

The coroner turned and said, "Welcome, I have some new info for you."

They went to the table, but Sarah and Walt both held back by the door. Dave came up and said, "What do you have?"

"Well, at first, I presumed this person was homeless, but I have to revise my statement. After doing my prelim autopsy and examined the stomach content, this woman ate very well. Not at all like a homeless person who would hit a shelter and eat processed foods. There were remains of steak, pork and lettuce, which doesn't decompose quickly in the stomach. So she had to have had a good breakfast. Some potatoes also. Also her nails were well taken care of; she cleaned and filed them regularly or went to a nail salon. Long speech short, I'm saying this woman was not homeless. Oh, and she was in her late seventies."

"Anyway to identify the body?" Warren asked.

"Well, I still have more examining to do, x-rays and tox. I'll have more, hopefully, tomorrow."

"Thanks Doc, give me a call when you're finished." Dave said.

They left the building and headed back to the cars.

Dave stood looking to the building, "So she wasn't homeless. Who was she? Did he bring her here from Seattle or Tacoma? Olympia is closer. Or did he grab her here? Not many women in this area who lived alone for him to kill, without drawing suspicion. Unless..." he paused.

"What, you know someone?" Warren asked.

"Could be a long shot, but follow me." They got into their cars and drove out, as the Toyota sat down the road from them, waiting. The man started his car and followed carefully.

Dave drove up just past the burned out rental house and over to another road. They arrived at a house off the road, behind a tangle of tall growing brush, and parked in the drive.

"Mavis Brinn lives here. She's a recluse since her husband ran off with another woman. They were all in their Seventies, so I guess age doesn't matter who you love." They went to the door as Dave knocked. "Everyone stand back please, she's a little mean and may bring a shotgun to the door."

Fatal Departure

Everyone but Dave moved down the steps and to the ground. Warren was ready to draw his weapon, if needed. Dave knocked again and tried to look in the window next to the door, it was covered with paper. This surprised him, he signaled to Warren to come up on the porch.

"I've been out here before, when she made a complaint about trespassers. She didn't have paper on the windows."

"The rental house did, didn't it?" Warren replied.

"Yep, so now I'm thinking that Mavis could be our body in the morgue." He turned to Walt and Sarah and told them to go back to the car, and asked Walt to protect Sarah. They moved away as Dave went to another window and it was also covered with paper.

"Okay, I have probable cause to enter, if she is alive and complains. Shall we break in?" Dave said.

Warren hit the door with his foot and it splintered easily being old wood. Dave stuck his head in the door and looked up, no box. He glanced around the room and saw no flashing red lights. "Maybe the killer only had one bomb?" Dave said.

They entered, Dave calling to Mavis, no answer. "She never leaves this house, if she not asleep in her bedroom, I'd say she's our body."

They went to the kitchen and stopped. The kitchen table was covered in plastic and there was blood on it.

"Okay, we've identified our body."

112

~~*~~

Watching from down the road, the man sat in his car cursing his luck. They found his hideout too quickly. He now had to find a new place to set-up and start again. Luckily he hadn't unpacked his car, so he left nothing in the house to give him away, just the set-up where he decapitated the woman. He left her head in the refrigerator to use later, but they would find it now, too bad. He pulled his map again and studied it; maybe he should just go to a motel. No, it would be too hard to carry a body in and out. All the rental places would now be watched, so that was out. He saw a campground, no, not a good idea. He decided to leave town long enough to explore another thought. He started his car and headed out to the 101 South to Olympia.

~~*~

Two hours later, the State Police forensic team was at it again. The supervisor, Al Lawson, said, "We're going to start billing you guys for all these calls," he laughed.

"Al, have you gotten anything from the other crime scenes?" Dave asked.

"The guy was good, left no evidence anywhere. We're still examining what we found. If we get anything good, I'll call personally just to stop this guy from creating more crime scenes. Oh, and the bomb at the rental was generic, made from common household items, except the C4, he had to have brought that in. He must have had experience with bomb making."

"Thanks Al. Keep me informed." Dave said as he led Warren out of the house. "This is now getting too close to home. He also needs to find another base of operations. We need to get ahead of him. Let's warn everyone about any strangers moving around town. Get everyone involved. Time for a town meeting."

*

Chapter 16

Back in the station, Dave went to the desk phone to call the Mayor. Before he could dial, Warren's cell phone buzzed and he answered. Dave waited to see what it was about. Warren listened to the person on the other end, he was frowning. He hung up and said, "Not good news. The check we sent proved nothing. They found the prints of the landlord and a few bank people. There were no other prints that they could pull off it. The name on the account was not our killer since the account was closed due to the person who actually had the account died a month ago. So that avenue is closed. Also, that was my supervisor calling and he has to pull the men at the stakeout back to the city. They think they have a terrorist cell developing in Seattle and they want all agents on alert. He said Walt and I could stay, since he's getting pressure from the Police Commissioner to find this killer. They still think it's the same killer from Seattle and they want retribution for the death of the detective."

"Okay, I'm calling the Mayor and I'll see if we can get cooperation from the town to watch for him." He picked up the desk phone and dialed. After a few moments he said, "Ken, this is Dave. I need to talk to you. Got some time now?" He paused and then continued, "Great, we'll be there in ten minutes."

He hung up and looked to the clock on the wall. It was now just before four, he said to Warren, "I'm going to ask Walt if he'll drive Sarah to the old house to get her car. He can bring back your agents to their vehicles. They can leave now, while you and I go talk to the Mayor. Sarah, come back here and wait for me."

"Works for me, Walt take charge of that." Walt nodded and took Sarah and Van Gogh to their van and left.

"Shall we visit City Hall?" Dave smiled.

They drove over and found the Mayor in his office. "Hi Dave, how's the case going?"

Dave thought it was strange that the mayor hadn't heard all the gossip, or he was just trying to start a conversation. "Ken, this is FBI Special Agent Warren Stevens, Warren, this is Mayor Ken Harris." They shook hands. "I wish I had better news to bring you, but I don't. Mavis Brinn was a victim of the killer." The Mayor looked shocked. Dave continued, "We need to mobilize the town to help with this. Get everyone involved in watching for the killer. Any strangers loitering or any houses that are suddenly being used that weren't before. Can you call a town meeting so I can speak to everyone?"

"I'll call Louie Diehl at the radio station and have him put out a call. That's the fastest way to do it, then the

115

gossip line can take over. Call Lois Carter, she has a big mouth," he said with a grin.

"That will work. Let's make it for tomorrow night, since it's too late now. Let me know how the response is. I'll start the ball rolling at the Halfway House, most people end up there." Dave said and then filled the Mayor in on what had happened the last few days.

They finished up and left, going to the restaurant and leaving word for the wait staff to pass along. They went back to the station and saw that the van of the extra agents was gone, and Sarah's car was back now.

"So, did you talk to the Mayor?" Sarah asked when they came in.

"Yep, we're having a meeting tomorrow night at City Hall in their community room. Now we just have to hope the killer holds off on anymore murders. Hopefully, since we took away the latest base of operations from him, he'll have to regroup. That could take time."

"I'm ready to go home, if you have no more pressing things to do?" Sarah asked.

Dave looked to Warren, he shrugged, and said, "I got nothing."

"Okay, Virgil should be coming in soon to relieve you, Mike. Tell him to call me if he hears anything, no matter how small."

"Sure Dave. Sarah, will you be in tomorrow morning?"

"For a short while, then I need to go see a doctor," she replied.

Mike thought for a moment, "You sick or pregnant?" he asked.

"Mike! That's no question to ask a woman," Dave exclaimed, "No, she's not pregnant. So just leave it at that and keep it to yourself, or all the gossips in town will be passing on that info. Let's go," he said to everyone and they left.

Sarah put Van Gogh in the car and told Dave that she'd be right behind him. Warren yelled that he would take up the rear to watch for a tail. Dave drove his Bronco out, followed by the caravan of cars. He took the long way around again, not knowing that the killer wasn't even in the town.

~~*~~

In Olympia, the man drove around looking for just the right place. He found one off the main highway and drove about a block down from the RV lot he spotted. He parked his car where he figured it would be safe and walked back to the lot. He came in from the side, away from the highway so he wouldn't be seen. The lot was closed now, it was after six, and he hoped they didn't have any security guards. He found just what he wanted and worked on the door lock of the small Winnebago motorhome. He was inside now and looking around. It would do for what he wanted and he could move around with it. What with all the tourists driving through the town, he would blend in. He hot-wired the thing and drove off the lot, down to where he left the car. It was a stolen car anyway, so he didn't worry about it sitting here. He moved all his personal things into the motorhome, wiped down the car for prints and then drove off, back to Brinnon.

~~*~~

They arrived at the house and in to relax for the night. Everyone was tired so they all passed on watching TV and just headed to bed. Warren and Walt went to their cots and relaxed. Dave and Sarah went to the bedroom and undressed to sleep.

"Do you really think this man is after you?" Sarah asked when they were tucked in.

"We figure that's the link as to why he's even here. He's leaving no messages or anything to suggest outright that he's after me, but we deduce that's the reason. We just have to play it by ear and see where it goes. I called a friend back in Tacoma and asked him to do a search on the few cases I was on there, to see if anything pops for why someone would have a grudge with me. He said he'd call when he's done."

Sarah was quiet for a while as they lay in each other's arms. "What would you say if I did tell you I was pregnant?"

She could feel Dave tense up, "Are you?" he asked nervously.

"No, I'm just asking. How would you feel?"

He paused thinking, pulling his feelings out, "I'd be crazy happy. I've always thought about a family. The fruitcake bitch I lived with didn't want children, she was afraid it would ruin her figure and she didn't want to take care of a baby. So, of course if you were pregnant, I would be terribly happy."

"Terribly happy?" she said raising her head to look at him.

"Okay, bad choice of words, but you know what I mean. I'd be ecstatic, joyous, delighted, enthused…"

"All right I get it. Terribly happy." She snuggled back into his shoulder, "Just don't get yourself killed, or you may not become a father."

"Are you sure you're not pregnant?"

"I think I would know, dear. I'm not."

They were both silent, thinking of the pitter-patter of little feet. Sarah was asleep shortly after, Dave just laid there thinking now about the killer. "Bastard", he said quietly.

The next morning, Monday, everyone was enjoying breakfast and there had been no calls during the night, so all was well. So far.

"I'm going to call my friend in the Tacoma P.D. and see if he came up with anything on my past cases." Dave said as he munched on a sausage biscuit that Sarah had microwaved.

Fatal Departure

"You think getting the townspeople involved will help?" Walt asked Dave.

"Well, if they all band together, it might make him do something foolish. We need to make him uncomfortable enough to be stupid and get caught," Dave said swallowing the last of the biscuit.

"You need to get everyone to band together in groups and watch their backs now." Warren offered.

"This is a small town, nearly everyone knows everyone, so that should be easy." Dave's cell phone buzzed and he went off to the living room to answer. It was his friend in the Tacoma PD calling.

"Don, I was going to call you today. What did you find?" he said hopefully.

"Not a damn thing. All of the men you sent away are accounted for, either in prison or dead. Although one is living in Florida and has alibi's for the last month. So I can 't find any connection to your cases here. Sorry pal. If you need help taking down this creep, let me know. I have some vacation time and would be more than happy to help."

"Thanks Don, I'll let you know. Talk later." They finished the call and Dave stood looking out to the waters of the Hood Canal. It was calm. Dave thought, like the calm before the storm.

*

Chapter 17

"I can drive myself." Sarah said, after they arrived at the station.

"I know you can, but I'm not taking any chances. Virgil will go with you to the Doctor's office and hang with you. Well, not in the room with you and the Doc, but nearby. I don't know if the killer will go after you to get to me. So no argument, Virgil goes with you."

She paused and then said, "Alright, I understand your feelings. I'm glad you have Warren with you now. For protection. So Virgil can be my bodyguard."

"Good, now we can both relax." Dave turned to Virgil sitting at his desk and said, "Virgil, if anything happens to Sarah, don't come back."

"You got it boss. When do we go?" Virgil asked.

"I am supposed to be there at one, so we can get lunch first and then go to the Doctor's office, if that's alright with the boss?" she said with a smile.

"Sure, I'll even buy lunch, just don't get anything more than ten dollars." Dave replied, then he and Warren went to the conference room followed by Walt.

Mike was still at his desk, "So I have to pull a double shift, so you can go play bodyguard?" he said to Virgil.

Fatal Departure

"We need someone to take the calls, you are the best for that." Virgil replied.

"Oh, and you are the big shot cop now while I'm just the office boy?"

Dave came back out the door and yelled, "Don't even start arguing now! Virgil, take Sarah and go for a ride until lunch. Mike, take calls. Enough, I'm not babysitting you two." He went back in the room as Virgil stuck his tongue out at Mike, who didn't see him.

Sarah giggled and said, "Shall we go?"

Mike was grumbling after they left, when the phone rang. "Sheriff's office," he said then listened. He stood, holding the phone and yelled to Dave. "Got a call for you Dave."

Dave came out and took the phone, "Hello, Sheriff Chandler here." He listened, "Okay, thanks."

He looked to Mike after hanging up, "Forensics is at a dead end, this is getting annoying.

~~*~~

The man drove the motorhome right through the middle of town, past the fire house and over to the road that led to the RV park. He went into the office and registered, using a fake ID that he bought in Seattle months ago. One of three he could use. He pulled his motorhome into the space and got out looking around. He had chosen a lot that was away from the other lots, saying he wanted privacy. He went back in and down the short hallway to the bedroom in the back. He stood looking at the body of the bum he picked up in Olympia, lying on the bed, now dead.

~~*~~

Sarah and Virgil had enjoyed their lunch and were sitting outside the Doctor's office about fifteen minutes before she was due.

"So Virgil, do you like being a cop?" Sarah asked.

"It's not bad, I was a security guard in Tacoma for a couple years, but that was just boring sitting around watching businesses. This job has a little more action to it, especially since the killer came to town."

"Are you from Tacoma?"

"No, I'm from here originally, my parents moved to Tacoma when I was twelve. Lived there until Dave moved back here with the crazy woman, I followed him shortly after to work in my Uncle's bakery. Dave and I were good friends, I had hoped to get on the Sheriff's team, so I waited for a opening. Dave helped."

"Dave is good people isn't he?"

"Yes, he is." They saw a man coming out of the Doctor's office, Sarah looked at her watch, it was almost time.

"May as well get this over." She got out of the car, leaving Van Gogh, and up to the front door, Virgil was two steps behind her. She stopped and said, "Are you going to follow me inside?"

"If I don't watch you carefully, Dave will be pissed."

"Okay, but you wait in the lobby." They went in and found Doctor Gladwin talking to her receptionist. The woman looked to Sarah and her escort entering and smiled.

"You must be Sarah Keller?" she asked.

"That would be me. And this is my bodyguard, Virgil." Sarah replied.

"Yes, I already know Virgil." She nodded to him. "How are you doing today, Sarah?"

"I'm doing great. Is that the whole thing, are we done?"

The doctor laughed and said, "I'm afraid not, we have more to discuss, if you'll follow me." She turned to go in to her office. Virgil said he'd wait out in the lobby.

"Please have a seat," she said pointing to an easy chair next to her. Instead, Sarah went straight to the wall covered with diplomas and certificates, reading them.

"Are you checking my credentials?" Gladwin asked with a smile.

Sarah turned, "Just making sure you didn't go to medical school in Jamaica or South America. I'm impressed with all the awards you received." She said looking to the framed papers.

"I have been busy, yes. Now shall we sit?"

"No couch?"

"No, I like people to feel at home, not ready for bed. It's easier to relate when you are facing each other."

Sarah went to the chair and sat across from the doctor. "So how do we do this? I've never been to a shrink… sorry, psychiatrist before."

"Just relax and we'll get to know each other first. I understand you are from New York, what made you move out here in the country?"

She sat back thinking, "The murder of my husband. I was a wreck living in the house he was murdered in, and going through the paces of trying to forget. I guess I figured moving as far away as possible would help. It sort of did."

"How so?"

"It was a whole new world for me. I was a big city girl and living here was a culture shock. It brought me to a whole new perspective. The people here were so different than in the city, nicer, friendlier but a little too nosy, especially Lois Carter."

Gladwin laughed out loud, then composed herself and said, "Yes, I know Lois well. So was the move beneficial for you?"

125

Fatal Departure

"At first it was hard, getting used to the change. Lois tried to make me feel comfortable and it was working. Then I met Dave, Sheriff Chandler."

"Yes, I also know Dave."

"Yes you do, don't you. Sorry,"

"That's alright. How was your relationship with Dave at first?"

"Slow, Lois was trying to push us together and I resisted. I like making my own moves and when someone pushes, I resist. But I was trying to forget my past. I dearly loved my husband, we knew each other for years even before we were married. I needed to heal, to get over it, life goes on and all that. I think Dave provided a rebound romance at first. I needed closeness, a man to make me feel like a woman again and not the empty shell that I became. He did just that. As we got to know each other, I developed a loving bond with him."

"How long before you met Dave was your husband murdered?"

"It was about seven months. What would you say is a good amount of time to heal from the loss of a love?"

"It depends on the circumstances, in your case, it depends on your strength to get past it. Dave filled a need that you longed for, correct?"

Sarah thought on that, "I was frustrated not having a man in my life, so yes, he filled that need. But he became more than that. He's kind, gentle, caring and loves life; and I'm sure he loves me."

"So from all you've said, your life is going well now?"

"Yes, I'm happy. We still have to work out a few details, like a place to live. The house we have now is really run down, but we are temporarily living back in the house where the killers nearly got me. We're hiding out."

"Yes, from the serial killer. Hopefully he won't find you out there in the woods" Gladwin said with a smile.

"We're being careful about it."

"Tell me about the dreams?"

"Oh, yes. The reason I'm here. Well, they started about a month ago. I dreamt about my husband's murder along with my best friend. The blood and everything. Then I felt someone coming after me, that was the horrible part. I screamed and Dave woke me."

That was the first, how many have there been?"

"Three, the last was when I was napping this past Friday. I was in a library, and the books were attacking me then there were three monsters coming for me. Again, I screamed and Dave woke me. My knight in shining armor." She smiled at the thought.

"Did the dreams start after or before you started your book?

"After, I was writing it about a month before the dreams started."

"Are you still working on the book?"

"I've put it aside for the last few days. I'll get back to it later."

"Have you had any dreams since you stopped writing?"

"No, but I don't think it's the book doing this. I don't forget things easily. I often have flashes of the murders in my head, during the day. I wish I could erase them from my mind, but I see or hear something that triggers the memories."

"Are you going to start writing again?"

"I will after this mess with the new serial killer is resolved. I don't need anything more to worry about. I moved out here to get away from crime and it's just not letting go, is it."

"No, it doesn't look that way."

*

Chapter 18

"Have you given any thoughts to moving back to New York?" Gladwin asked.

"There are things there that I miss, like a good deli, but I'm happy here. No pressures to be perfect here, and I've made a few good friends."

"What bothers you, in your everyday life?"

She thought about it, then said, "I really don't have much that bothers me. Even with this killer running around, I'm not really upset too much."

"Why do you think that is?"

"You tell me, you're the shrink." She said with a grin, "I think that the incident at the house with Harcourt and the Slasher, I've seen the worse there. So how much worse can it get? Besides, I have Dave and the FBI around to protect me."

"You seem to have it together, but we really need to find out what it is that triggers the bad dreams."

"Well, I would say all the crime I've been exposed to. The first dream was about my husband's murder, the next was me running from the killer in the woods. The last was about books, I think it was my desire to get away from editing books for others. Maybe it will end now."

"Good. Well, we have just touched on the subject today, more of an introduction. I don't want to push too much, too fast. So if you'd like to come back next week this time, we can see how things are going. As you say, the dreams may stop, but everyone has an occasional nightmare. Let's hope yours will lighten up."

Fatal Departure

"Okay, this didn't hurt too badly, I'll be glad to talk more. Thank you."

"Please, if you have more dreams, write them down and when they happened. And anything that came up during the day that may have set it off."

"I can do that. Are we finished?"

"As I said, today was just an introduction, we can go into more detail if you need it next week. Yes, we are finished, so go rescue Virgil and we'll talk again next week."

They stood and went out to the lobby. Virgil was talking to the receptionist, then saw them come out. Everyone said their good-byes and Sarah left followed by Virgil.

They went back to the station and Dave came up to Sarah, he was studying her head. "What?" she asked.

"Your head seems about the same," he said looking serious.

"What are you talking about?" she asked again.

"It's not shrunk any, so I guess your appointment went well."

She hit his arm and went past him with Van Gogh. She sat at the desk that Mike had vacated when they came in the office. He checked out and went home quickly, before they found more work for him. Van Gogh sat next to Sarah. She sat back in the chair and said, "I did good, she wants to see me next week and I'm supposed to write down any more bad dreams."

"I hope you don't have any more bad dreams, but if you do make sure I'm around to kick butt."

"I'll be sure. Now don't you have a town meeting to organize?"

"We have everything under control. The word has spread like wildfire, especially since Lois was informed. The Mayor called and said he's getting a large response from the radio announcement. Warren and Walt went to get some food and then they will be back to join us for my big debut on stage."

"That I got to see," she said with a smile.

~~*~~

The man had finished preparing the body of the homeless man in its bag and then cleaned up the bloody plastic in the motorhome's bedroom. He put the wrapped body by the side door and went to the driver's seat. He backed out of the camp lot and drove out onto the road leading over to town. He had already found a place to dump this body earlier on his way through town. He got to the 101 and down to where the General Store was and pulled along the side, with the motorhome blocking the view. He got out and looked around to be sure no one was watching and quickly dragged the body down the stairs and set it up next to the dumpster on the side of the building. He looked around again and then got back in the driver seat and quickly drove away. He was looking in his side mirror at the body standing against the dumpster and smiled.

~~*~~

The community room at the City Hall was packed to capacity. There were still people standing outside who wanted to come in but there just wasn't any more room to allow the extra people. Dave had a speaker set up out a window so the people outside could hear what was being said. The mayor was sitting on the small platform and was waiting for Dave to start.

Dave went to the podium and turned on the switch of the microphone. There was a squeal from the speakers so loud everyone yelled. Virgil turned down the gain on the amplifier and the squeal stopped. Dave tapped the microphone a couple times, then said hello into it. The sound came through the speaker just fine.

"Okay everyone," he said as he looked to Sarah sitting in the front row. She was going to be his focus as he hated being in front of crowds. "I need your absolute attention and no questions or comments until I say so." The crowd was silent, Dave was glad for that.

"I'm sure everyone here knows that there has been a rash of bodies dumped in our town. We believe that this is the work of a possible serial killer from out of Seattle. I have two FBI agents here," he pointed to Warren and Walt standing off the side of the platform, "Agents Stevens and Meyers, and they will be helping to track down this killer. But we need your help also. We don't have any idea what the killer looks like so he could be any stranger traveling around our town. I'm sure everyone here carries a cell phone now, so please have them handy. I need everyone to be vigilant about watching for anything unusual going on, some person loitering or a building that was not being used, now occupied. The killer needs a base of operation to do his work."

He looked to Sarah and she gave him a wink. He continued, "As most of you know, Mavis Brinn was a victim of the killer, but she was the only local person to be murdered. The other bodies came from outside our community. We don't need any more of our citizens murdered, so I ask everyone to watch each other, go out in groups if you can, or call someone to join you if you have to go out alone. If we band together, the killer will back off of taking another life here. Now I don't want anyone, and I repeat anyone, playing hero and attacking every stranger you see." This got a laugh, Dave relaxed a little more.

"We get a good number of tourists and campers going through here, and using the campgrounds. They need to use the town for food, gas and supplies. We're sure this person is working alone, so ignore groups of people. I'd like Special Agent Walt Meyers, an FBI profiler with the Seattle Behavioral Analysis Unit, to come up and talk about what to look for." He turned to Walt and the man came forward. "It's your turn, Walt." he said and went to stand by Warren to listen.

Walt cleared his throat and said, "Ladies and gentlemen, the FBI and the Seattle police are quite sure this killer is one we endured about two years ago, doing the same as he's doing here. Back then, it was determined that the killer had a vendetta against a detective in the Seattle Police Department. The detective was eventually murdered and the killings stopped. We are quite certain that this killer has his sights on your Sheriff." That brought mumbling from the crowd.

He continued, "The FBI BAU in Seattle has developed a possible profile on the man. We estimate he is now in his late thirties; tall, we estimate from prior evidence; very strong by having in the past being able to attack homeless persons without a weapon, usually breaking their necks and he may exhibit signs of agitation. He would be very dangerous, so avoid contact. If approached by any person you are not sure of, move away quickly or yell for help. It usually scares them off. As the Sheriff said, travel in groups if possible, never alone in public or places where you can't escape." Walt turned to Dave and quietly went off the platform. Dave went back to the podium.

"Okay, any questions?" Dave asked, but before he could continue, his cell phone buzzed. "Excuse me, please." He stepped away from the podium and answered, listened, then looked to Warren, he nodded. He went back to the podium and said, "I have to cut this short, please be cautious now, alert to anything and be safe."

He left the podium followed by Warren and Walt. Sarah came around the crowd and out the door behind them. They all arrived at their cars and Dave turned, "We have another body, dumped by the General Store. One of the employees went to empty some trash and found the body leaning up against the dumpster. The big thing about this is the killer finally pinned a note to the body."

*

Chapter 19

The store clerk was standing outside the building keeping people back from the crime scene. He looked out to the road as he saw the Sheriff's car flying up the highway with siren and flashers. Dave pulled up to the side of the building the clerk was pointing to. All the spectators moved back as Dave and Virgil exited the car. The black Van driven by Warren came rolling in just after and then Sarah in her Vibe came shortly behind them. She parked on the other side of the building so not to get in the way. She got out with Van Gogh and went around to where they were.

Virgil was calling for everyone to get back and then pulled the yellow tape from the trunk of the car and started to surround the area with the tape. Dave asked the clerk to explain what happened.

"I was bringing out the trash from the store and found it, just standing there next to the dumpster. I didn't touch it, but I did go close enough to see an envelope taped to the thing. It was addressed to you Sheriff. I didn't touch it either."

"Are you sure you didn't see any activity over here? A vehicle stop or someone loitering?"

"No Sheriff, nothing. I was busy in the store getting ready to close."

Fatal Departure

"Okay Martin, just go back in your store, close it but don't leave yet. We'll take it from here."

The man nodded and left. Dave and Warren went to the body and looked to the envelope. It read, "To Sheriff Chandler only, personal!!"

"Let's not touch anything until forensics gets here. I had Virgil call them on the way here. I told him to tell them this was a priority one, we finally had a note." Dave said.

Warren was looking around the ground, it was messy with trash. Dave said to get everyone back for now. They stood waiting for the State Police forensic people to arrive as Dave was pacing, wanting to know what the note said. About twenty minutes later he could hear the sirens and the van came down the road being led by a State Police cruiser.

They both pulled up and the team got out and came to Dave. He showed them the crime scene and they went to work, taking pictures and examining the bag.

The State police investigator got out of the cruiser and came to Dave, "So we got a note, maybe we'll have an answer now."

"I'm hoping so Charles, I suppose you came out to see what we had?"

"Yeah, I was in the station when the call came in. I decided to join the forensic team and see if I could get a take on it."

"Well, we won t know until we read it." They stood watching the men gc over everything.

After they finished taking pictures for the record, one man pulled the note from the body and carefully opened it. He had the photographer take pictures of the open note and then they put it in a large plastic sleeve. The man handed it to Dave. Everyone gathered around him as he read it out loud.

"Sheriff Chandler, I hope you've enjoyed my little presents. I wrapped them just for you. Of course they were missing a few body parts, but I'm saving them for a special occasion. To put around your lifeless body. In case you're wondering why I'm coming for you, you'll have to figure it out. I'm not giving away any trade secrets, to get myself killed. Oh, and watch that cute little girlfriend of yours, she won't escape from me, I won't screw up on that. Your friend, the Slasher."

"What the hell, the Slasher is dead, I know because I shot and killed him." Dave spoke.

"That was the NY Slasher, this guy must be copycatting him. It happens in many cases where a killer is idolized enough that a copycat emulates him," Walt said. "This guy isn't even emulating the NY Slasher properly, he kills, removes body parts and bags them. The NY Slasher tied his victims to a chair, and slashed their throats. The two aren't even similar. He's just using the name."

"Fine, this is some nut job pretending to be his hero." Dave said with some agitation.

Fatal Departure

Warren put his hand on Dave's shoulder and said, "Dave, look at the note and examine it. He said he's not giving away any trade secrets. What kind of trade secrets? Then he threatens Sarah and says he won't let her escape from him, he won't screw that up. Who did she escape from that he won't let it happen again?"

Dave studied the note and looked to Walt, "What's your take Walt?'

"I see the same inferences that Warren does, he's giving you clues, maybe not deliberately, but he's bragging and telling too much." Walt said.

Dave thought about it and said, "Okay, the only people Sarah escaped from were Harcourt and Draegon, AKA the NY Slasher. She escaped from Harcourt because of the Slasher and I stopped the Slasher from killing her. This guy knows the story, it's been all over the news. So he figures that he will finish the job that was prevented."

"As good a theory as any other. We don't know the identity of the killer but we know his plan." Warren said, "We may need to get Sarah out of town until we catch this bastard." Warren said.

"I'm not going anywhere, I'm not running so don't even think it," came Sarah's voice from behind them. Dave forgot that Sarah was even following them, he was so wrapped up in reading the note. He went to her.

"Babe, if we take you out of the equation, it will mess with his plan. He will have to go after me then." Dave replied.

"I don't care, I have the best team of law enforcement to protect me, and I'll never be let out of sight, so I'm not worrying. I'm not leaving you."

"I probably will regret this, but I'll let you stay. But… you have to have a bodyguard. No arguing. It's firm."

"Who? Virgil?" she asked.

"Nope, I have a better person. You'll meet him tomorrow." He turned to Charles, the State Police investigator, and handed him the note. "See what you can get off this and get back to me."

Charles handed the note off to the forensic leader and said, "Do your magic and get something."

The coroner's van pulled up and Doc Norris got out. "How was fishing?" Dave asked him.

"Lousy, and too short, you got another body I hear. Aren't you getting tired of this?" he replied.

"Yes, and this body had a note attached."

"Really? Did it say he was going elsewhere to play?"

"Nope, but he is definitely after me. And Sarah. So we need anything you can get from the body."

"I'll do my best," he said and went to the corpse.

They spent another hour and everyone had done what they could, finishing up. Sarah told Dave that she had an appointment tomorrow with a reporter, so she wanted to go home to rest.

"Do you really need to be interviewed?" Dave asked.

"It sounds like fun, and I get to promote my book."

"You're still going to write it?"

"I'm getting close to finishing it, so yes. I need every bit of publicity I can get."

"Okay, but I will be having a bodyguard on you now. So be aware of it."

"He better be good to keep up with me," she said with a smile.

The State people left and the coroner had removed the body, the store was now closed, and it was finally quiet. Dave, Sarah and the men stood by their cars. "I'm hungry, shall we go get some food at the Halfway House?" Dave asked. Everyone agreed. They all got into their cars and went to the restaurant. Later, Dave dropped Virgil at the station and drove home, taking the long way again.

They all settled into the house and Sarah said she was going to bed. She left the living room where the men were enjoying their beer.

"So who's the bodyguard you're going to have watch her?" Warren asked.

"An old friend of mine. He's been a little on the other side of the law, but I trust him. Besides, he knows that I'll shoot him if he screws up." Dave said with a smirk.

The next morning, everyone staggered out of their beds. Dave was already up and making coffee. Sarah came out of the bedroom looking like she was the Wicked Witch of the West. She hadn't combed her hair and looked green around the gills.

"Do you need to clean up for our guests?" Dave asked.

"No, they can just take me as I am," she smiled and kissed him on the nose.

"You will clean up for the reporter?"

"Yes, of course. That's important, you people are collateral damage." She sipped the coffee and went back to the bathroom.

Dave went to the door when the bell rang. He opened it after peeking through the hole and smiled. "Good morning, Bruiser," he said to the rather large, muscular man standing in leather gear looking every bit like a biker. He was about a head taller than Dave and totally bald, with a goatee. He had tattoos all over his arms and one earring in his left ear.

"Why do you call me Bruiser? My name is Clarence," he said with a growl.

"Bruiser sounds more dangerous than Clarence. I need you to be dangerous, so Sarah will relax while you protect her. So I'm calling you Bruiser."

Dave brought the big man in and introduced him to Warren and Walt, just as Sarah came out of the bathroom.

Her eyes grew large when she saw the huge man standing before her. She looked to Dave and said, "My bodyguard? I like."

*

Chapter 20

"Sarah, this is Bruiser. He's a bond enforcement agent in Tacoma and a good friend." Dave said.

"A bounty hunter? Wow, I've never met a bounty hunter. So you are going to protect me?"

"It will be my pleasure, Missy. I shall not let anyone get near you." The mountain spoke.

"Okay, everyone you've met Bruiser, now, this is FBI Agents Warren and Meyers," he said pointing them out. "We need to investigate the case and I won't have to worry about Sarah now, will I Bruiser?"

"You got it Chief, I am on the job."

"Do you still carry that cannon of yours?"

"It's under my vest, always by my side." Bruiser said with a smile showing perfectly straight teeth, all shiny white.

"Good, just don't shoot Sarah. Now gentlemen, shall we go to work and catch a murderer?"

They all went off to get ready to go as Sarah walked around Bruiser, checking him out. "So how many bail jumpers have you caught?"

"I've got a 92 percent recovery rate, it's in the hundreds. They don't get far from me."

"You have a badge to do this?"

He reached in his back pocket and pulled the wallet, flipping it to the badge. She studied it and smiled. "Okay, I have an appointment with a reporter today at one, in a nearby restaurant. So I'll let you know what is happening when it happens."

"Works for me, just let me know."

Sarah said, "I have to finish getting ready, you don't need to follow me while I change clothes, do you?"

"No Missy, I'll just keep an ear out for your screams."

Sarah laughed and went to her bedroom. The men all gathered in the vestibule, Dave giving Bruiser last minute details and they left. Sarah came out and asked, "Did Dave leave?"

Fatal Departure

"Yep."

"Without a good-bye kiss? I'll have to have a long talk with him," she said with a sly smile.

"He's got a lot on his mind. This fool killer is rattling him. I've known Dave for many years, and he's usually not upset by many things."

Sarah led him to the kitchen and offered him some coffee, he accepted. "How did you meet Dave?"

"He busted me, during a gang fight. I used to be part of a small motorcycle club in Tacoma and we had a run in with a rival group. The police arrived and Dave managed to take me down. Any man that can do that is aces in my book. Later, I quit the gang life and Dave got me a job with Ace Bail Bonds. We've raised a few beers over time and then he moved away. I come out here every so often to visit."

"Nice story. Since I've been with Dave, he's never been much of a buddy kind of guy. He really has no friends other than Virgil."

"Virgil Whitefield? Yeah, he's good people too. If you need a friend who will stand up for you, Virgil is one. I don't get out here as much as I like, so we don't see each other much. My job keeps me busy, the world is full of bad people."

"Tell me about it," she said as her phone rang. She answered and it was Terry Buscemi, the reporter. "Yes Terry, what's up?"

"Just checking to see if you are still coming today," she asked.

"I'll be there, with a friend. He may be a little overpowering, so don't be startled. See you at one."

They finished and hung up. "Too bad you warned her about me, I like startling people," Bruiser said with a smile showing those perfect teeth again.

They drove up the highway to the restaurant, about fifteen minutes early. Bruiser wanted to scout out the area and the restaurant before the meeting.

Sarah waited in the car, with the doors locked, while Bruiser skulked around the building. Sarah thought it was a bit overkill, but she admired the man's determination to do his job.

She was startled by a knocking on her window, looked up to see Bruiser. She thought he was good to have slipped up without her seeing. It also worried her that the killer could do the same. She opened the car door and got out.

"Looks good, no one loitering, or watching that I could see. If this guy wants you, he will want to grab you and take you away so to torture Dave. I'm not worried about him shooting you from a distance, but it doesn't hurt to be cautious."

"Thank you, Bruiser," she said as she started towards the restaurant.

"May I ask you a favor?" he asked.

Fatal Departure

She stopped and turned, "Sure, what?"

"Call me Chaz, my real name is Clarence, but I use Chaz. Dave was just trying to create an image of me being dangerous by calling me Bruiser. Not the first time he's done that."

She gave him a wide smile and said, "Of course, Chaz. I like it better than introducing you as Bruiser anyway." She turned back towards the door and they went into the restaurant. The people inside were eyeing the big man, but he was with Sarah, so they relaxed.

Clara, Sarah's favorite waitress, saw her come in and went to her. "Who's your friend, Sarah?"

"Clara, this is Chaz, he's a bounty hunter. So don't jump bail or he'll have to track you down. Chaz, this is Clara."

"Wow, he'd be worth jumping bail for," Clara said looking up to the huge man.

"Sorry, I don't hunt women, only men. So you'd be safe." Chaz grinned.

"Darn, well, you two need a booth?"

"I have another person coming, so could we have one away from people? She's a reporter and wants to interview me."

"Oh neat, you're going to be in the paper?"

"We'll see, if all goes well."

Clara led them to a booth towards the back, secluded from the other diners. She dropped menus and went to get water for them.

Sarah was watching the door, even though Chaz insisted he face the door. She didn't know what Terry looked like, but figured if a woman came in with an over-sized purse, it probably would be her. About five minutes later a blond female, slender and attractive came in. Clara went to her and they spoke a moment then Clara brought the woman to Sarah and Chaz.

"Here's your reporter, Sarah," Clara said.

Chaz stood and startled Terry. He smiled and let her slip into the booth. Chaz pulled up a chair from a nearby table and sat at the end of the booth, still facing the door.

"I want to really thank you for this interview. I'm not taken seriously on the paper. They just want me to cover weddings and other crappy events. Getting your story will help me get some credibility," the woman said.

"I'm glad to help, Terry. This man is my bodyguard, Chaz, also known as Bruiser. He's a bounty hunter in real life, but my boyfriend asked him to watch me until they catch the serial killer lurking around here."

"I've heard about that. I'm surprised the paper hasn't sent someone over here to cover it." Terry said.

Fatal Departure

"Well, maybe you can hang around and get that story also. I'll talk to Dave, my boyfriend and he's also the Sheriff, and I'm sure he'll be happy to talk to you."

"Oh my god, that would be so great. This is going to be a big break for me."

"Okay, how do we do this?" Sarah asked.

Terry took out a small recorder from her over-sized purse along with a note pad with pen. "Well, I ask questions and you answer. It's simple enough. Shall we start?"

For the next two hours, they talked as Clara kept bringing them coffee and finally a big plate of fries. Clara brought Chaz his own plate of fries, he smiled at her and said thanks.

Sarah's cell phone buzzed, she excused herself and answered, it was Dave. "How's it going, babe?" he asked.

"Very nicely, Terry is very pleasant and efficient. Have you caught the killer yet?"

"We're still sifting through everything, but he will screw up and we'll get him."

"I'm glad you're confident about this, but I feel so much better with Chaz nearby."

"Chaz? What happened to Bruiser?" he said, but Sarah could tell he was laughing.

"Never mind Bruiser, you just need to worry about leaving this morning without kissing me good-bye."

"Oops, sorry about that. I'll make up for it tonight. I just called to see how everything was going, and if Chaz was working out. So I'll let you get back to your big moment. Talk later." He hung up and Sarah put her phone away, looking to Terry, "I'll talk to him later about you interviewing him. He'll either agree or I'll make his life miserable."

"I don't want to be a troublemaker. If you even think the Sheriff may be against this, don't even ask."

"Terry, you have to be aggressive if you want to be a good reporter. You have to go after the story, even if you feel otherwise. Dave is a good person and would be more than happy to answer any questions you have," Sarah said.

Chaz spoke, "I've come in contact with a number of reporters in Tacoma, after I brought in some criminal. They all bugged me enough to get me to talk about a case. I really couldn't tell them much, just that I caught the missing person, I don't get involved with the case. But they were smart enough to go after every lead, for the story. Just don't make things up and get your facts straight."

"Never question Chaz. Just go with your instincts." Sarah said.

"I'll try. Now what can you tell me about this new serial killer?"

*

Chapter 21

Sarah laughed, "You make it sound like we have frequent serial killers here."

"Sorry, as I said, I'm new to this. What is going on with this person, how is he doing his crimes?"

"He's been murdering homeless people and dumping their bodies around our town. He did kill one local woman, but Dave thinks it was a killing of convenience, he needed her house and she was in the way. Dave and the FBI now know that the killer is after Dave. They don't know why, but he left a note finally, threatening Dave. And me. Which is why I now have the Incredible Hulk as a bodyguard."

Chaz laughed as Sarah continued, "We have no clue as to his whereabouts, but it will be a matter of time until he is caught. He has to be nearby, unless he's doing an awful lot of driving between here and Olympia." She paused to take a sip of coffee, then said, "For some reason he blames Dave for something in his past. He wants revenge, or so Dave feels. The State Police forensics team can't find anything at the crime scenes to give him away, he's very careful not to leave clues. I wish I could tell you more, but that's all I know."

"Well, it's enough to write a lead in, I can then talk about past serial killings in Seattle that may be connected to this." Terry said as she was writing on her pad.

"Oh, yes, the FBI and the Seattle Police think he may be the same killer that stalked Seattle about two years ago. They're trying to connect him to those murders."

"I remember that, he dumped bodies and then killed a police detective. It was so sad, then he just disappeared."

"Yes, and it concerns me that with the entire Seattle police around they couldn't stop him from killing the detective. So what are Dave's chances?"

Chaz spoke up, "Hey, don't talk like that. Dave is cleaver and smart. He wouldn't let anyone near him he didn't want. Now that they know his intentions, they'll be careful."

"Thank you Chaz. I appreciate your confidence in Dave. Now, Terry are you about finished?"

"Oh I'm sorry, it is getting late. I have enough now, to at least start my story. Let me know what the Sheriff decides about talking to me, will you?"

"No problem. Well Hulk, shall we go?" Sarah slid out of the booth as Chaz pushed his chair back to the table. They all said their good-byes, then Sarah asked, "Are you driving back to Olympia or staying around here?"

"I have a room at the Bayview Motel. I'm staying the night and going back tomorrow, unless you can get me an interview with the Sheriff."

"I'll try. I have your cell number, and I'll call after I talked to him."

Fatal Departure

"Thank you, hopefully we'll talk again."

They went out and Terry got into a red Corvette. "Nice car," Sarah said to Chaz as they went to her Vibe. They drove out and to the Sheriff's office. After they parked, they went in and Dave saw Sarah coming down the hall. He went to her, grabbing on with a big kiss.

"You'll have to do better than that for not kissing me this morning." She smiled and walked past him.

"Where's Van Gogh?" Dave asked.

"I left him home, I didn't know how long I was going to be in the restaurant."

"Hope he hasn't torn apart the house." Dave said and walked into the conference room.

Chaz followed Sarah to the desk where Sarah sat. He sat on a chair next to her. "You probably have spent a lot of time in police stations?" Sarah asked Chaz.

"Yes, just visiting. Only once under arrest." He smiled.

Virgil came out of the conference room and saw Chaz. "Clarence! How the hell are you?"

"What did I tell you about calling me Clarence?"

"You'd kick my ass, but I'm a deputy now, so it would be assaulting an officer," he grinned. "Sarah, how'd your interview go?"

"Good, are you guys any closer to finding the killer?"

He looked back to the door and said quietly, "Nope, we are at a standstill. Dave is going to organize an all-out assault on the town. We are going on a door to door search. All over the area. It will probably take a few days but it's the only thing they can think of."

Dave came out and stopped at the counter, "Chaz, how's your day been so far?"

"Excellent, I had two beautiful women in my company. Free food and being chauffeured around, not a bad job."

"Has Sarah filled you in on our problem?"

"Yep, while we were driving around. You're trying to find his work place, where he cuts up his victims."

"Yes, and we've shut down a couple of his places. We need to look for his new base."

"Maybe he doesn't have a base, at least not one stationary. Back when the gang I ran with was going out to stir up trouble on a road trip, we took an RV. It's mobile, and a place to crash. You've got campgrounds in the area, check them out."

Dave was quiet then turned and went back to the conference room. "I guess you got him started," Sarah said to Chaz.

Fatal Departure

The three men came out of the room and Dave yelled to Virgil to follow. Dave stopped long enough to ask Sarah to watch the office. She agreed. They all went out.

"Now what shall we do?" Sarah asked Chaz.

"Do you know how to play hangman?" Chaz said with a smile.

~~*~~

The man had pulled the motorhome to the side of the party store across from the campground and got out. He went around to the front of the store when he looked to the road, just as the Sheriff's car and the black van drove by heading into the campground. They hadn't seen him due to the angle of the building, hiding the RV on the side. He watched them drive up the dirt road to the office and everyone got out. They went into the building and the man decided it was time to dump the RV. He went back to the motorhome and drove out quickly. He thought it was lucky that he saw them. It would be hard to outrun the cops in the big motorhome. He thought about it and decided to take the thing back to Olympia to a place he knew where to hide it, so no one would find it for quite a while.

~~*~~

Dave and his friends talked to the manager of the campground, he gave them a rundown of who had motorhomes and what lots they were parked. They went out and drove around in Dave's car.

Bob Moats

"This makes sense, it's mobile and it's roomy. Perfect for a killer on the loose." Dave said as they approached the first RV. They pulled in as the door opened and out stepped a boy of about twelve. The men got out of the car and Warren called to the boy. "Are you with your family?"

The boy stopped and asked, "Who wants to know?"

Warren figured the kid was being a smart ass since they were in a Sheriff's car and Dave had his uniform on. Warren pulled his badge and said, "FBI, wise guy, now are you with your parents?"

A man came out the door and looked startled. "What's going on?"

"Are you traveling with your family, sir?"

"Yes, my wife, daughter and son. Why?"

"Nothing, sorry to bother you." They got back in their cars and drove around to the next lot. It was vacant. "Let's go on to the next," Warren said.

After examining all the motorhomes in the campground, they decided if the killer was traveling this way, he had to have been the one from the one vacant lot. They went back and pulled the card on the pole that identified who was camping there. It had a name, probably fake, and it said only one person in the lot.

"One man alone, it fits. But where is he? There's one more campground he could have moved to, but he could also pull off into the state forest and disappear easily." Dave offered.

155

Fatal Departure

Walt spoke, "True, but this doesn't make sense, we could easily spot an RV moving around since we know now. Maybe he's through with it. Maybe he's left town to regroup. I'm sure he would not figure on using the RV for his whole stay in town."

"So, we are at another dead end? This is just great. Let's go roust the RV's on the road. Maybe he's still driving around."

As Dave got into the car, his cell phone rang. He answered and listened, then hung up. "That was Virgil, he just got word on his investigation into the first body we found, the one dumped in the grave. He checked with a number of tattoo parlors close by and got nothing, so he called a friend in Tacoma to see if he could find anything. He sent a picture of the tattoo to him and he just called Virgil back. He couldn't find any parlor in Tacoma that recognized the tattoo so the friend sent the picture to another friend in Seattle Police. They checked with the parlors in the city and located one shop that had the tattoo on file, they have to keep copies of what they do. It was done about two and a half years ago, it's a tattoo of a special forces unit logo during Viet Nam. Here's the kicker, it was listed as being put on a man by the name of Ron Trombley. Our missing FBI agent."

*

Chapter 22

"That's impossible. Trombley disappeared two years ago, if this was his body it would be really decomposed by now. Unless, the killer kept him in a freezer for two years." Warren said.

"Or Trombley wasn't dead, just hiding out for some reason. I'll check with the bureau to see if there's more to it." Walt added from the back seat next to Virgil. He pulled his cell phone and made a call.

"It makes a bit of sense to me; the killer put Trombley into the grave, thinking it would be buried with the coffin. Unfortunately it rained and spoiled his plans. He wanted to get rid of Trombley's body." Dave said.

"But why cut off the head and arms if he was figuring the body wouldn't be found?"

"You just had to make this harder, didn't you?" Dave asked.

"All in the line of duty." They sat as Walt was mumbling in the back seat, then he finished.

"I talked to the Director, he's glad to have the body found, but he will get back to me on something I asked of him." Walt said as he finished his call.

"What?" asked Warren.

"I'll let you know when I get word."

Fatal Departure

"Sure, keep us in suspense."

"I like a little mystery, and if my idea has merit, I'll tell you."

The men spent the next two hours pulling over RV's on the roads, finding nothing. They wore down and headed back to the station finding Sarah and Chaz playing darts on the board that was on the back wall.

"Good to know my town is safe from crime with you two on the job," Dave joked as he came in.

"Hey, we're just the office help. You are the crime busters. Any luck?"

"No, but we did find out the first body in the cemetery was our missing FBI agent Ron Trombley."

"But I thought he vanished two years ago?" Sarah asked.

"Yep, that's the mystery. Walt has an idea that he's checking on, so we may still have something. Has Mike come in for his shift yet?"

"He's in the men's room making himself look pretty," Sarah laughed.

"Well, when he gets out, let's leave, I'm bushed and want to crawl in bed."

"Sounds like a winner." Sarah said as Mike entered the room.

"Hey, how did your RV round-up go?" he asked.

"Nada, we're regrouping, and going home. So hold down the fort. Any bodies, call. Chaz, you're with us right."

"You offered your couch, so I'm ready," Chaz answered.

They all left and went to the Hood Canal house and in to crash.

Dave made a quick salsa dip and put out a big bowl of Nacho chips. Everyone was sitting watching TV as Dave said he wanted to sleep and excused himself. Sarah said she'd be in shortly and looked to Warren.

"I think you wore him out. Stop doing that."

"He's a big boy and knows his limitations. Besides, I think he wants you to join him." Warren said with a smirk.

Sarah thought for about two seconds, then said, "Excuse me, but I'm suddenly tired. Good night gentlemen." She went off quickly, followed by Van Gogh.

Warren laughed and said to Walt, "Those two were made for each other."

Chaz said, "I've known Dave a good long time, he gets easily hooked on a woman, but they are always the wrong woman. At least this one is going to be good for him." He turned to Warren, "Did you know Farrah?"

Fatal Departure

"Oh yeah," he laughed, "I just talked to her last week to see if she had anything to do with this mess, she's really gone to pot, and not the illegal kind. She's gained weight and looks a mess. Luckily, she didn't have anything to do with this, I'd hate to have her back into Dave's life." He stood, "Well guys, I'm off to bed myself. I want to be fresh for the man hunt tomorrow. Good night." He left the room followed by Walt.

Chaz looked around and then took the blankets and pillow that Sarah brought out and got on the couch. He left the TV on to watch a movie that was showing, but dozed off shortly after.

~~*~~

The man had arrived in Olympia and drove the RV over to where he left the Toyota. Surprisingly, it was still there. He drove the RV past the car down the drive now covered over with weeds and pulled into an abandoned factory parking lot. He drove the thing around the side and parked. Closing it up he walked back to the car and got in. He had left the keys in the glove box and recovered them, starting up the car. He sat a moment before driving the car to the RV to get his personal things, thinking about his next move. It had to be spectacular, something that would really get to Dave. Something to really hit him hard. He thought about Sarah. Now was the time to go for it.

~~*~~

It was dark in the cemetery; the leafless trees were all reaching out and swaying in the wind, now kicking up. The moon was the only light to illuminate the hallowed grounds. Sarah walked quickly, weaving through the

160

headstones, trying to find the way out, but with every turn she was back at the middle. She felt the chill from the wind, cold and blowing worse now. She suddenly heard a howling. It was getting louder and moving towards her. She turned to see two glowing red eyes watching her. They moved to her left and she turned to run. She ended up back where she started and then the eyes were all around her. Every tombstone had eyes now, glowing in the dark, blinking blood.

She turned again and ran into something standing in her way. She backed up and waited until her eyes adjusted to the low light. It was a body standing, with no head. Her mouth opened but nothing came out. She turned to run again but every direction was another headless body. They were coming towards her now. She was stepping backwards to get away, but suddenly fell back into a hole in the ground, a grave site hole. She looked up at the bodies standing all around the opening high above.

They were swaying in the wind and suddenly all of them started to drop down into the hole with her. She was trying to avoid their bodies as they fell, but it was hurting and she was suffocating from the weight. She now let out a scream that pierced the darkness, when she felt a slap.

"Sarah, wake up!" Dave was calling as he turned on the bedside lamp. She sat straight up and screamed again as Dave took hold of her. The door to the bedroom flew open and there stood Chaz with his .357 Magnum out.

"Chaz! It's alright. She's had a bad dream again."

Fatal Departure

Chaz aimed the gun down and said, "Boy, she has a pair of lungs, I about fell off the couch when I heard her the first time."

Behind him, Warren and Walt came flying around the corner. Dave called them off. "Thanks guys, go back to bed, she'll be alright shortly."

Everyone went back to their rest, as Dave comforted Sarah, still sobbing. She pushed back and said, "When is this crap going to end? I'm sick of it, it's all too real."

"What was it this time?" Dave asked gently.

"It wasn't Harcourt or the Slasher, it was the cemetery and the headless bodies now. I'm moving into the present crimes now. Can I just get past it?"

Van Gogh had jumped up on the bed and Sarah grabbed on to him, hugging him tight. "I want Van Gogh in bed with us."

"That's fine with me, maybe he'll give you some comfort." He paused, "Do you think you can lie back down?"

"Just leave the light on."

"I will, now rest, you've had the bad dream, so hopefully you'll be alright for now."

"I'm okay. Go to sleep, you need the rest to catch the bastard invading my sleep." She laid back as Van Gogh plopped down next to her, she hugged him. Dave laid back and he knew he wasn't going to sleep well tonight.

Around seven, Dave was up getting coffee. Luckily Sarah had gone back to sleep and rested quietly the morning. Everyone came out and Dave put the pot of coffee on the dining table so they could take what they wanted.

"How's Sarah?" Chaz asked.

"Sleeping again, hopefully peaceful. Thanks for rushing to our rescue. I know I can count on you."

"Hey, it's what I do for my friends."

"Thanks."

Warren got his cup and sat at the table. "What's the plan for today?"

"Damn if I know. We can try the house to house search but I think it's useless. So I guess we just wait for him to make a move. I hate to have another homeless person killed, but what can we do?"

Walt was seated when his cell phone rang, he answered. "Hello? Yes, I understand, hold on." He handed the phone to Warren, "It's the Director."

Warren cringed a bit, then took the phone, "Yes, sir, Agent Stevens here." He listened for a while and was nodding his head. He said, "Thank you sir, I'll get on it and let you know what we find." He hung up and handed the phone back to Walt.

163

Fatal Departure

"It turns out that Trombley didn't just disappear two years ago, he's been way deep undercover with the mob."

*

Chapter 23

"The mob? Trombley was deep undercover with the mob? We may have a hitman here." Warren said.

"Warren, does the mob hire serial killers to do their hits for them?" Dave asked.

"Actually most hitmen are serial killers, in a way." Walt said, "They enjoy killing and have people to hit. So it's a perfect job for a serial killer. Plus, they get paid for it."

"Okay, so all these homeless bodies were bumped off for the mob? Along with Trombley?"

"No, they probably were collateral damage. This guy evidently was hired to hit Trombley and then went freelance to drive you crazy." Warren added.

"Great now we have a hitman running loose." Dave said as he turned to Chaz, "Be extra careful now."

"He won't get past me," Chaz said confidently.

Dave sat and asked, "How does one go undercover for two years? That's an awful long time to investigate any mob."

"I've known of a few agents who were undercover for more than that. They establish themselves in with the mob and we keep them there as long a possible. Plus, they can jump from one mob to another, keeping us informed of activities and movements. It's not unusual. Trombley came up missing because he had to establish a whole new identity to join the mob."

"Wow, I'd hate to give up my life to live with a bunch of gangsters." Dave said.

"They do return to normal eventually. Unfortunately Trombley won't be returning," Walt spoke now.

"Can you find out what mob Trombley was involved with, maybe they can find out who their hitman was." Chaz said.

"Not a bad idea," Warren said, "Walt give a call back to Organized Crime and see what they have. Call the Director if they balk. You seem to have a direct pipeline to the boss."

Walt was quiet, then said, "He's my Uncle." Everyone looked at him with surprise.

"I just knew you had an inside to get on field work. Not that I didn't think you could handle it, but…"

"I understand. I'm not the toughest agent in the field. but I have the smarts." Walt defended.

Fatal Departure

"Yes, you do Walt. You've gotten us further in our case than Warren has." Dave smiled, as his friend gave him a dirty look.

Walt stood and said, "I'll go get the information." He went out of the room to call.

"Give the little guy some credit, he has helped us." Dave said before Warren could speak.

"Okay, I'm just a little in awe of him, he's brainy and I'm just a big old dummy. I have the brawn but he has the brain."

"Pinky and the Brain." Chaz said with a grin, referring to the cartoon mice. Pinky was a dumbbell mouse and Brain was a mouse always trying to take over the world.

"I love you too Chaz." Warren shot back.

"Before you two start sparring, let's wait and see what Walt finds out. Are there actually mob activities in Seattle? I wouldn't figure there would be a mob there." Dave asked.

"We call them the Starbuck Mob, it's a joke on the fact that we found out they drink tons of coffee. They're actually part of the D'Amico mob out of LA. They run prostitution and gambling in the city. They are bigger than the homeboy gang mob that runs the streets and harasses businesses for protection. We've been watching them for years but actually haven't gotten any solid leads to take the big boss in LA down. We have raided their activities here, but they always get off, good lawyers - best dirty money can buy."

Dave said, "Of course. How do you find a lawyer in a tank full of sharks?" No one answered. "He's the one scaring off the real sharks." No one laughed, but Chaz gave a groan.

"That's bad, man," Chaz said.

Walt came back and said, "They are checking with OCU to see who is on the roster for the job of hitman. They said they'd call back."

"I suppose Organized Crime knows all the players?" Dave asked.

"They do, unless the mob brings in outside killers to do the work. It disassociates them from the murders. But they can check with the main FBI Database from other states for names. It takes time."

"So what do we do now, go fishing in the Canal?" Warren asked.

"Let's go into the station and wait to see what the killer throws at us next. Not much we can do until we get word. Maybe even a picture of the hitman."

"If he's in the database, they should have a picture," Walt said.

"Unless he's a loner. He may be off the radar totally." Chaz mumbled.

167

Fatal Departure

Dave stood, "Whatever, we can't sit around here all day, we have citizens to protect." He left the room to go get ready. Everyone else followed slowly.

Dave woke Sarah to tell her he was leaving. She stretched and reached up to him. "I love you," she said with a kiss. He smiled and kissed her back.

"I love you too. Chaz is in the dining room. Get dressed so he doesn't get antsy." He stood and left the bedroom.

The men left leaving Chaz still sitting. Sarah dragged herself out to the kitchen but the coffee was gone. Chaz called from the dining area saying the coffee was with him. She took a cup and sat at the table pouring the coffee into her mug. She looked rough.

"Tough night, eh?" Chaz said.

"Thank you for rushing in, I'm glad to know you are alert," she said sleepily. She took a sip of coffee and made a face. "It's cold."

Chaz stood and said, "I'll brew a fresh pot." He took the thing to the kitchen and started the coffee machine back up.

"Anything new on the case?" Sarah called to him.

Chaz came back in and said, "As a matter of fact, Ron Trombley, our missing fed, was actually an undercover agent with the mob."

"Really? That's new. So our killer killed an undercover agent. Did he know he was undercover?"

"We don't know yet, Walt is running down a few leads. Trying to find the identity of the hitman."

"Hitman? Now our killer is a hitman. This just keeps getting better." Sarah smiled and went to the kitchen for the coffee.

Chaz asked, "What have you got going today?"

"First, I'm going to clean this house after the mess you pigs made. Then we can go in town to harass the cops," she said with a big grin.

"I'm for that." Chaz went to the living room to help clean up.

~~*~~

The man smiled at his cleverness. He sat right by Sarah Keller and the reporter in the restaurant as they talked about her adventure with crime. He knew what to expect, since Sarah gave a brief explanation of what the police were up to. He also knew what he was going to do next. He steered the Toyota up towards the Bayview Motel and pulled on the side of the office. He went in to register, using one of the three fake ID's he had, then went to his room. He was satisfied with the conditions and went back out. He sat in his car waiting for the reporter to come out of her room, so he knew where to find her.

~~*~~

Fatal Departure

The three men sat in the conference room, just waiting. Virgil returned from the store with a box of donuts and a carry tray of steaming coffee cups for everyone.

Virgil set the food and coffee on the table and said, "What now?"

"We wait. Walt called again about the hitman and was told they have a lead on one guy. They are going to send a mug shot of him when they locate it. If we have a photo it will be easier to spot him."

Sarah walked into the room, straight for Dave. She gave him a kiss on his forehead and said, "Can I talk to you out in the lobby?"

Dave looked at her suspiciously and said, "Okay." They went out. Chaz was loitering at the counter talking to Virgil. Sarah led Dave towards the entrance, and turned to him.

"I have a big favor to ask. I made no promises, but could you talk to the reporter I talked to yesterday about this killer? She's fair and could use the push with her paper." Sarah asked then waited.

"If I say no, are you cutting me off of sex?" he said with a sly smile.

"I hadn't thought of that, but it works for me." She laughed, "I just didn't want to step on your feelings about being interviewed."

"I appreciate that, but it's a good idea actually. If the killer reads the paper it may make him do something that will help us, something stupid."

"Great, I'll call Terry and let her know you will talk to her."

"Tell her to come in this afternoon, after we have more information from the FBI." He kissed her and went back to the conference room.

Sarah pulled her cell phone and called Terry. It rang a while until her voicemail answered. She left a message and hung up. She wondered why Terry didn't answer. Maybe she was taking a shower, that could be it.

She went to Chaz and said, "Let's go take a ride." He stopped leaning on the counter and followed her out of the station.

~~*~~

The man walked around Terry Buscemi, tied to the chair, her mouth taped shut. He had finally seen her come out of her room to do something at the office. He waited till she came back and went to her door, softly knocking. She opened the door and greeted him. He stepped forward pushing her into the room, pulling a gun and telling her to keep quiet. She did. He told her to go out of the room, hiding the gun in his jacket. He took her to his room where he had everything set out to bind her to the chair. Now he would have his fun.

*

171

Chapter 24

"Where are we off to?" Chaz asked, as he sat in the passenger seat of her Vibe. The car was small but roomy, even for the huge man.

"I'm driving up to the Bayview Motel to tell Terry that she can talk to Dave. I called, but she didn't answer, I want to catch her early enough," she said.

They drove up to the motel on the shoreline of the Hood Canal. It had a beautiful view of the water. Sarah pulled in and parked. She saw the red Corvette that Terry drove and went to the office.

"Morning Sarah," the elderly man behind the counter said as they came in. He eyed Chaz with suspicion, but Sarah introduced him.

"Sam, I need to know what room Terry Buscemi is in. I called, but there was no answer. I need to talk to her."

The man looked into this register and said she was in room 8. Sarah thanked him and they went out. They got to room 8 and Sarah banged on the door, hard.

"Trying to wake the dead?" Chaz asked.

"She may be in the bathroom, I want to let her know we are out here." She banged again. The door to the next room opened and some man was yelling about all the noise, then he saw Chaz and went back in quickly.

172

"It's nice having you with me, you intimidate people," Sarah said.

"I enjoy intimidating people," he grinned

She knocked again quieter this time. "Strange, she should have answered by now."

Chaz reached past her and grabbed the door knob, it turned and the door opened slightly. Chaz told Sarah to stand back and he pulled his Magnum, pushing the door open with it. He stood off the side of the door in case someone planned to shoot. He peeked around the corner and saw no one in the room. He entered carefully and checked the bathroom.

"It's empty," he said.

"Something is wrong, her purse is on the dresser and her car is out front. This doesn't look good." She pulled her cell phone and called Dave, explaining what she found. Dave said to wait and be careful, then he hung up.

"Dave is on his way."

Chaz said, "Stay in the room and lock the door, I'm going out to look around the place." He went out and Sarah closed and locked the door.

Chaz carefully went around the parking lot, checking all the car license plates, two were from the Seattle area. He knew this from his bounty hunting job, plates have numbers that tell where they are issued. One car was a Cadillac and the other was a Toyota. He looked into the cars, the Toyota had a lot of clothing and personal things stacked in the back, it was a mess in the front, coffee cups and papers all over the seat and floor. It looked like a person had lived out of it for a while. The Caddie was clean. He watched the room windows, for sign of movement, but saw none. He went back to the room and knocked, telling Sarah it was him. She opened the door and he stood just inside, still watching the parking lot.

About five minutes later, the Sheriff's car pulled in followed by the FBI van and parked. Dave and the two FBI agents got out and came to the room they saw Chaz standing by.

"Talk to me," Dave said to Sarah when she came out. She told him what had happened when they got there. They went in to the room and Dave checked Terry's purse. He found the tape player and note pad, along with some personal things. There was a good deal of money and credit cards, so it couldn't have been a robbery.

"Any possible way the killer could have known Terry was here for you?" Dave asked.

"I don't know, she may have told someone, but we just met in the restaurant yesterday and talked."

Dave turned to Chaz, "Did you see anyone looking suspicious in the restaurant?"

"There were lots of people eating, no one looking out of place." He thought back, then said, "There was one man sitting fairly close who was there a while, but I didn't think much of him."

174

"It could have been him. But why does he want the reporter?"

"Insurance," Walt said. "If we get too close, he can use her as a pawn to escape."

"Sure, hide her and then we have to find her while he skips out." Warren added.

"Well, that means she wouldn't be murdered, thankfully." Dave said.

"Poor Terry, she's just a society reporter, not a big deal crime reporter. Why would he want her?"

"She was someone important to you, it was personal," Dave replied. "I think this is aimed at you."

Sarah's cell phone rang, she looked to the caller ID, it was Terry's phone. "Terry's calling, I'll put it on speaker." She answered and pushed the speaker button. "Hello, Terry?" she spoke.

"Sorry doll, but your friend is a little tied up at the moment," came a male voice from the speaker. "Now listen real close, I have her and you won't get her back unless you do what you're told."

"You son-of-a-bitch, if you harm her, you'll regret it." Sarah yelled.

"Shut up and listen!" the voice yelled. "I'm going to make you regret what you've done, you and your boy toy, the Sheriff. I'm in command now, you'll just have to wait it out, before I do my final execution of you both."

Fatal Departure

Chaz went out of the room and walked along the front of the old motel, listening to each door. He couldn't hear anything until he got to the last door on the end of the building. He heard a voice sounding agitated and talking loudly now.

Warren had seen Chaz leave the room and came out the door. He saw Chaz with his ear at the door he was by. Chaz turned and saw Warren, signaling to him to come. He said something back into the room and went down to Chaz. Walt stuck his head out the door and then came halfway down the front of the building and stopped.

Warren listened to the window of the room. He could hear what sounded like the voice on the phone. He pulled his service revolver as Chaz pulled his Magnum. Chaz banged on the door, then there was a volley of gun fire from the room. Luckily they were smart enough not to stand in front of the door or the window.

They backed away as Dave came flying up. The door opened and a voice called out, "Back off, I got the woman. If you want her alive, back way off."

"You can be a fool, if you kill her how long do you think you'll live?" Chaz yelled.

There was no reply. It was too quiet. "Hey fool, what is it going to be?" Still no reply, they waited.

It was just enough time for the killer to slip out the back bathroom window and run into the woods behind the motel.

"Crap!" Dave yelled, "Go to the back of the building. I'll bet he's going out that way." Chaz and Warren were the first to sprint around the building. Dave came to the door and peeked in carefully. Terry was still tied to the chair. He could see through to the bathroom, the window was open, the bathroom was empty. He rushed in and cut Terry loose. Sarah had been outside with Walt and then they came into the room. She saw Terry stand and went to her, they embraced.

"I thought I was dead when you guys came to the door. After all the shooting, he stood near the door, then went to the bathroom and climbed out the window."

Chaz came back in and said, "He's gone, out into the woods. We could chase all day and not find him in there."

They took Terry back to her room and she sat on the bed. She told them what happened and then Dave said, "You've seen his face, he'll not let that go. I'm surprised he didn't shoot you while he had the chance."

"If we had heard a gunshot in the room, we would have attacked figuring he shot Terry. He knew that while we were waiting for an answer and Terry was still alive, he could slip out quietly." Warren offered.

"True, we'll need to protect both Sarah and Terry now." He turned to Sarah and said, "Looks like our home is becoming a bed and breakfast."

Walt came back in the room, "I checked with the manager and got the info the killer left with him. Probably fake, but I'm having it checked now. The Toyota was his car, we can have it checked for prints and may get a lock on him through that."

Dave spoke, "I already called the forensic team to come look at it. We were just so close on this, but we have him on the run now, and without a car."

They waited for forensics to show up and then Dave had Sarah and Terry follow him to the station in their cars, to regroup. Walt and Warren stayed with the forensic people to be sure the killer didn't come back.

Dave's car radio crackled with Virgil's voice. He answered, "Go ahead, Virg."

"Got a call from Greg Ferris, someone stole his car from his driveway. Are you going to check it out?"

"Won't do much good, it's long gone by now. Have Greg come in to file a report for insurance, if we don't find the car."

"Okay, over and out."

Dave spoke out loud to himself, "This guy moves quickly, too quickly."

*

Chapter 25

Dave arrived with Sarah, Chaz and Terry at the station. Virgil said, "Greg Ferris isn't happy, he has no car to get into file a stolen car report."

"A Catch-22 situation. Virg, go out there and take the paperwork to him. Maybe that will make him happy. He should have a new car by tomorrow, if his insurance company is any good." He turned to his followers and said, "We need to relax and go over a few things. Let's go to the conference room."

He opened the door and everyone went in. "Now, tell me everything from the meeting yesterday at the restaurant."

Sarah spoke first, covering the whole meeting, up to leaving the restaurant. Chaz gave his side of it and then Terry spoke about what she did and saw. Dave said he was going to call Clara at the restaurant to see what she knows about the guy sitting next to them. "Just relax, I'll be back shortly." He went out.

"Terry, how are you holding up?" Sarah asked.

"Well, for having a gun pointed at me and being tied up, I'm holding it together as best I can. Why is he doing this?"

"It's a mystery so far, he just says that we are bad people and wants to kill us." Sarah said with a smile.

Fatal Departure

"I don't see how you can be so calm about this?"

"I'm shaking inside, but I can't let Dave see it. I'm already seeing a shrink about bad dreams I'm having. Dave would lock me in a room with the shrink, if he knew how I really felt." She looked to Chaz, "Don't you even tell him that."

"Tell him what?" he simply said.

Sarah smiled as Dave returned. "Clara said she doesn't even remember the man. He left no record, like a charge receipt. So we have nothing there. Walt has requested the photo of the hitman from the bureau. We'll have Terry see if it's him."

Warren and Walt came in and Walt handed Dave an envelope. "What's this?" Dave asked.

"The photo of the hitman we assume is the killer." Walt said.

"Where'd you get it?"

"We have a communication center in the van. It came in through the computer to the printer."

"Nice to have federal money," Dave joked.

Dave opened the flap and pulled the photo, it was a bit grainy but the face was recognizable. He went to Terry and handed it to her. She took a big breath and looked at the picture.

"That's not him, sorry."

"Crap," Dave said. "Okay, Warren can you get a sketch artist down here?"

"Even better," Walt said, "Terry, come with me please."

She looked a little surprised and stood, "Is this going to hurt."

Walt laughed and said no. They went out followed by Dave and Warren. On the way to the van, Warren said, "You're going to like this."

While they were going out, Virgil returned with the paperwork for the stolen car. He saw everyone walking to the FBI van and followed.

Sarah and Chaz followed up behind as everyone stood by the open sliding side door of the van. Walt had Terry sit in a chair by the monitor of the computer as he made a call. The video came on the monitor of a man and Walt asked for the sketch artist. The man disappeared and came back with a woman and her computer drawing tablet.

"Wow, giving an artist rendering over the computer." Sarah said.

"Saves on travel time, and it's fast." Walt said when he heard her.

Fatal Departure

For the next forty minutes, they worked on the sketch and then the artist showed the finished drawing to the camera. Terry gasped, and said "That's him."

Walt spoke into the microphone and asked the artist to send a copy of the picture to them and have it distributed in the FBI system and the Seattle Police system for a BOLO. The woman agreed and they signed off.

Dave looked into the van and said, "How much is this thing, I'll talk to the town council and see if we can get one."

"You couldn't afford it," Warren smiled and walked away. Walt pulled the photo print from the printer and handed it to Dave.

He showed it to Terry and she nodded, "It's him."

Dave handed it to Virgil and said to make copies. Walt said, "Hold on," and typed a bunch of keys on the keyboard and then pushed a button on the printer. He had twenty copies in less than a minute. He handed them to Virgil. The photo even had text on the bottom, now asking to watch for this man and report him to the Sheriff.

Dave smiled and told Virgil to take them around town and put them up everywhere.

"Will do boss," Virgil said and went to the patrol car.

Walt said, "I'll have the bureau do a facial recognition on the photo to get an ID." He went back to the computer.

Bob Moats

Dave turned to everyone and said, "It's not that late, but I'm calling it a day. With Virgil putting up the photos, the killer may run now. We need to rest and talk about this."

"He's stolen a car, so he may already be out of town." Warren added.

"I'm sure he'll be back. He has a mission to accomplish."

Walt came back in and said, "They're running facial recognition on the sketch, but it may not come up as well as an actual photo, being it's only a drawing. We'll see."

"It'll be something to go with, put a name to the face." Dave said and looked to Sarah. She seemed to have something on her mind. "What's up in your little world?"

"I was just thinking about something the killer said on the phone. He said, 'I'm going to make you regret what you've done, you and your boy toy, the Sheriff.' Now what have we done that we will regret?"

"I've put a few men away for various crimes, you've only pissed off a writer. Unless there are more writers out there who want to kill you." Dave smiled.

"I don't know why anyone feels they have to murder us. Both of us. I can see murdering you, you're a cop, but I don't do anything harmful to people."

"Yes, and it's the second time he's mention a vendetta against you two," Warren added. "You've annoyed someone along the way."

183

Fatal Departure

"Whatever, let's close up and go home," Dave said. It was almost five and Dave figured it will be a slow night. Mike was in now and could take care of the station. He told Mike to tell Virgil when he got back, to go home, but be back to work early in the morning.

They all went to their vehicles and drove out. Dave took the short route to the house, the killer shouldn't be around, he figured.

~~*~~

The man sat down the street, after stealing another car from out of town and returning. He was extremely pissed that they screwed up his plot and took his car with all his clothes and personal things. He saw his car sitting in a fenced area by the station, they towed it in. Time to recover his property. He saw everyone leave and waited till it started to get dark, then drove over to behind the fenced yard. He carefully went to the six foot fence and climbed it. He ran to his car and pulled the keys from his pocket, but the door wasn't locked. He looked in the back and all his things were put in sealed evidence boxes, ready to be examined. How fortunate that they packed his things, so much easier to carry. He pulled out the boxes and tossed them over the fence, then climbed out. He took everything to the new car and then drove off. He wasn't finished yet, it was time to do this. To take out them one by one.

~~*~~

Bob Moats

Everyone was sitting in the living room feeding on pizza from the oven. Dave brought out the beer and became the hero.

"Do you really think he's left town?" Terry asked. "I'd feel a lot safer if he did."

"He has no extra clothes now and we've got his image being put up everywhere. I'd say, but I could be wrong, he's probably on his way back to where ever his home is. To restock. I think we'll have a quiet night." Dave said, hoping to comfort the woman.

"Where am I going to sleep tonight?" she asked.

Warren wanted to say with him, she was a looker. Sarah figured each man's thoughts and said, "You can sleep with me, Dave can sleep in the bathtub."

"Like hell, I'll get out the sleeping bag and air mattress from the patrol car and sleep in the living room with Chaz."

"Why do you have those items in the car?" Chaz asked.

"For stakeouts, good to be prepared." Dave replied.

"As long as you don't share that sleeping bag with anyone but me." Sarah threw in.

Walt's cell phone buzzed, he answered. "Agent Meyers speaking." He listened then pulled a pad out of his pocket and wrote on it. He thanked the caller and hung up. "Well, they got two faces identified. Since it was a

185

drawing, the details are missing, so they got two matches. One person is from outside Seattle, the other from Texas and he's in jail. So it's a good bet the mystery man's name is Frank Murdock. He's got a short sheet for a couple murders and he's beat each charge. Good lawyers and lousy busts."

"Frank Murdock, now we have a name." Dave said as his cell phone rang. He answered, listened, then hung up. "It seems Frank Murdock broke into the impound lot and took everything out of his car. He's back."

*

Chapter 26

Dave woke around five a.m., from his sleeping bag on the floor of the living room. The air mattress deflated enough to put him nearly on the ground, so he couldn't sleep very well.

He looked over to Walt standing by the window and told him to go back to bed, he'd stay up now. Walt went to the spare bedroom and Dave went to look out the huge window overlooking the Hood Canal. It always gave him a smile when he saw the water. It was raining out now, not hard, just a light drizzle. He went to the kitchen to start coffee, but there was a fresh pot on the counter. Walt must have made it, he thought.

Bob Moats

He poured a cup then went back to sit on an easy chair, next to the couch were Chaz was sleeping.

"Can't sleep?" Chaz said, without opening his eyes.

"Damn air mattress nearly had me on the ground. I don't sleep well on the floor, and I get tired of blowing it back up."

Chaz sat up now and said, "I've slept on plenty of hard grounds back in my biker days. We'd head out on the road and have to sleep many nights under the stars. We weren't too welcome in motels." He paused then said, "Thinking about Murdock?"

"Yep, wondering what he'll pull next." Dave spoke quietly.

"Well, we're getting closer to him now, at least we have a name." Chaz said, swinging his feet to the floor.

"Names don't catch murderers, just makes it easier to identify them. He'll screw up, they always do on long crimes like this. They run out of ideas, then get antsy about killing. He'll screw up."

"Let's hope so," Chaz stood and said, "I gotsta go potty." He laughed and went out of the room.

Around seven, everyone was floating out of their bedrooms. They were quiet this morning, thinking about the killer being back.

"What's on the agenda today?" Sarah asked Dave.

Fatal Departure

"Go into the office and wait. Hopefully the photos will help to track him down. Maybe some citizen will spot him and call."

Walt got a call and went out to the living room to answer. He came back and said, "They're sending an actual photo of Murdock. It's coming in on the van computer." He headed towards the door. Warren said he'd go with him, just to get some air.

The ground was wet from the rain, but it had stopped coming down. They went towards the van, Walt unlocked the side door and got in. Warren was looking at the ground under the van, it was dry from the van covering it from the rain. He walked around the van and noticed something strange. He flew back around and grabbed on to Walt and pulled him from the vehicle yelling to run.

They got about twenty feet from the van, when it blew sky high. It shook the ground and knocked the two men off their feet. The front door of the house flew open and everyone came out to see the van in flames.

Dave turned to Sarah and asked her to call the fire department before the fire gets worse. Walt and Warren came up to them as Dave asked what happened.

Warren said, "I saw that the ground under the van was dry, of course, covering it from the rain. I went around the other side and saw a streak of wetness going under the van. I figured it was from somebody crawling under it, dragging the rain with them. I bent down and saw the bomb attached to the frame. Luckily, I got Walt out in time."

"But how was it detonated?" Dave asked.

"Mercury switch, probably. It jiggled when Walt got in the van and most likely had a timer to be sure as many people were in the van before it blew. I've seen them before. Boy, the Director is not going to like this."

"Fill out a report and your insurance will cover it," Dave smiled, trying to make light of the situation.

"Oh, sure. Thanks for that. You call the Director and explain it to him." Warren said.

Walt spoke, "I'll call him, he doesn't yell at me." The man went off again to call.

"I don't suppose Walt got the photo before it blew?" Chaz asked.

"No time, he barely had the computer up and running before I pulled him out. They can fax it to your office."

"We do have a computer here in the house, you know. They can send it here and we can print it out on the printer." Sarah offered.

"They can send it to the computer at the station, it would be better going there," Dave offered.

"Works for me, I'll have Walt give them your e-mail address."

Sarah told Dave, "I called the fire department, they're on their way." He thanked her.

Fatal Departure

Walt came back out with a frown and said to Warren, "The Director wanted to thank you for saving my life. He also said the cost of the van will come out of our pay."

"I hope he was joking," Warren moaned, "That sucker costs close to a quarter million dollars!"

"He said he was sending another unit down, but we had to sign for it this time. He wasn't joking about that," Walt said, and went to the flaming van to watch it burn.

About ten minutes later, the fire trucks pulled in and the men were working to put the fire out. The Chief came over and said to Dave, "You like playing with crazies who use bombs. This is the second one in a week."

"Yep, we just have the right kind of friends. I'll call forensics in to make the exam. You guys can take a break on this."

The fire was out and they stood looking at the twisted metal and parts all over the place. The fire department had left and the forensic team was just arriving. The supervisor got out and was laughing. "You guys have made history at the lab with this crime. We haven't been out to investigate this many crime scenes before on one case."

They went to work trying to locate the bomb parts. Walt wanted to pick up as many of the computer parts that he saw on the ground, but waited for forensics to release the area.

Dave's cell phone rang and he answered, listened, then hung up. "Virgil says he's getting calls now on Murdock. We need to get into town and follow up on them. Sarah, you take Chaz in your car, have Terry follow you in hers. I'll take Warren and Walt in mine. Stay close behind me." He stopped and then said, "Warren, check the cars for any other bombs. Just to be sure."

They arrived at the station and found a number of cars in front. "Great, now we have a mob." Dave said with a frown. Sarah pulled up as they parked and gave Van Gogh a quick walk to relieve himself.

They went in to find about twenty people all at the counter trying to speak. Dave yelled for them to shut up and then went around the counter. "Now, what is this all about?"

Virgil cleared his throat and said, "They all say they have seen the killer, and they are scared."

"People, this killer is not after any of you. He wants me, so just stay in groups and you know what the guy looks like now. If you see him, run like hell and call us. Now go out and let us work, please. But keep alert."

The crowd mumbled and slowly walked out.

"Thanks Dave, they were really getting to me. I don't like crowds," Virgil said.

"No problem. Now where's the sheet for the calls you took."

Virgil went to his desk and picked up the incident report and handed it to Dave. He studied it for a moment while everyone stood watching him.

Fatal Departure

"Wonderful, Murdock seems to be everywhere, and at the same time. It's now mass hysteria, so most of these reports are probably useless." Dave said, as he leaned on the counter.

Warren took the paper from Dave and read it, "Yep, the guy is everywhere. Murdock has his personal stuff back, but we don't know what car he's driving. It probably was stolen, why don't you check the police reports between here and Seattle for stolen cars, maybe we can spot it."

Dave turned his head to Virgil and said, "Get on that, see what reports you can come up with from the LEIN."

Virgil had to go out to the new patrol car to the device that gives data on the LEIN for reports of crimes involving stolen cars. Dave watched him go out and then asked Warren to get the photo from his office.

"I'll call," said Walt. He pulled his cell and placed the call. Everyone had drifted to the conference room, where Virgil had placed a box of fresh donuts.

"Yum, breakfast," Chaz joked. "Where's the coffee?"

"You can try ours, but I wouldn't recommend it, or you can go over to the General Store and get some fresh brewed." Dave looked to Sarah and said, "Why don't you take Chaz and Terry for a coffee run?"

"Sure, come on guys." She led them out as Warren asked if Dave wasn't worried about Murdock getting to them.

"Chaz will be watching for him, I'm not worried."

Walt came back and told Dave the photo had been e-mailed. Dave went to the computer and brought the photo up on the screen and punched the printer button. The printer spit out the photo and Dave added a few more copies. He handed the first one to Warren, as Walt looked over his shoulder.

"Ugly, isn't he?" Warren laughed.

*

Chapter 27

The man had watched the van explode. He was disappointed that the one agent had discovered his ploy. He used the last bomb that he brought from his home near Seattle. It would take too long to obtain another one, so he had to be more ingenious in his kills. He wanted the Sheriff and his woman to watch each person die, before he would take them out. He had to organize his plan now, it was getting annoying to let them live any longer. Even if he couldn't kill the others, he wanted his objectives dead.

He followed everyone as they had left the house, the forensic team still working on the van. He had followed them the night before to the new house, but he already knew about the place. It was part of his plan. He even had the lady Realtor show him the house before he made his first body dump. He wanted to see the house, and plan his move around the building. He was even able to enter the last house as a cable man. They would figure it was him, so they would move out and back to the Hood Canal house. The plan worked. He now had an idea to get the right people in place; he just had to make a phone call.

~~*~~

Dave had Virgil checking on the calls that seemed most likely good sightings of Murdock. They were back to the map on the wall, marking where Murdock had been seen. Dave stood looking at the pattern of sightings and said, "He's been busy. I guess he hadn't seen the photos of him around town before he did his daily routine. We haven't had any more bodies, thankfully, but he may start getting back at us since we messed up his life."

"Walt's outside waiting for the new van, they called and were on the way." Warren said.

"Try not to lose this one," Dave kidded. He turned to go out to the counter and see what everyone was up to. Sarah was sitting at Mike's Desk, Terry was sitting next to her typing on her laptop, and Chaz was nowhere to be seen.

"Where's Chaz?" he asked.

"He's out with Walt, and taking Van Gogh for a walk. Chaz wanted some fresh air."

Dave smiled and went to the front door, he wanted to look around the area, just for the hell of it. He went out the door and found Walt and Chaz sitting on the stone wall of the porch. They were talking as he came up. They saw him looking around.

"Watching for Murdock?" Chaz asked.

"I'm sure you would have seen him by now."

"I've been on the alert, if he's around, he's far enough to need binoculars."

They saw the black van driving up the road followed by a black Crown Vic. The two vehicles pulled up and parked in front of the building. Two agents got out and came to Walt.

"Special Agent Meyers?" One man asked Walt. Dave figured he looked like an agent of the FBI.

"Yes, I am. I've been waiting," he replied.

The man held out the keys and a clipboard, "Sign here." He pointed to the paper on the clipboard and smiled. Walt signed and then the agent said, "The Director said not to blow this one up." He laughed and the two men went back to the Crown Vic and drove off.

Walt went to the van and checked it out. He was happy to have his toy back. Warren came out and saw the van. "Did you have to sign for it?" he asked Walt.

"I did, it's ours now, so we need to be alert. I'm not paying for it." Walt climbed into the back and checked the electronic equipment.

Chaz said he was going back in to see what the women were up to. He left the others watching Walt play in the van.

Fatal Departure

Warren turned to Dave and said, "I thought Walt was going to cry when the other van blew up. He lives for gadgets. One of the reasons I like having him around, he knows how to use all that weird stuff."

"You're not a techie?" Dave said.

"I even have problems with cell phones, they don't like me. Walt keeps my grounded."

Walt stuck his head out of the van and said, "They sent the deluxe model, complete with GPS trackers. If we can get a module on Murdock we could follow him anywhere."

"Maybe even put a bell around his neck?" Warren said with a laugh.

"Don't make fun, this stuff is serious."

"Sorry Walt, I appreciate all you do."

Dave told Warren he was going back in, Walt said he was staying with the van. Warren followed Dave saying, "Walt will probably sleep with the van now. I'll have to set up a perimeter around the thing to keep Murdock from planting another bomb."

"I'm hoping he's done bombing. It's one thing I'm not fond of." Dave said as he held the door open for Warren.

They went back to the conference room, as Virgil was adding more dots to the map.

"Virgil, do you really believe that Murdock could have been to all these places." Dave asked.

"No, but you said to follow the leads. I personally don't think he was even in the town. We have so many tourists now, they all could look like Murdock."

"True Virg. Just add the calls that sound the best." He went out to Sarah and asked her to follow him. He led her to a store room, closed the door and turned to her. He pulled her to him and gave her a long, slow lip lock. After a few moments, she pulled her head back and said, "What brought that on?"

"I slept on the floor last night, I couldn't even snuggle with you. Smell your hair or touch your soft body. I was in hell." He smiled. "Was it good sleeping with Terry?"

She hit his arm and said, "Get your mind out of the gutter. Terry is a nice woman, but not my type. Now we need to get her out of here for her own good."

"I agree. I'll call a friend in the Seattle P.D. to come get her. They can give her protection, but I don't think Murdock will follow, he's busy here with us."

"Good, now I'll be able to sleep better." She gave him a sly smile and grabbed his ass.

~~*~~

The man sat in the car outside the office of the Hood Canal Reality. He had his cell phone up to his ear as he waited for the woman to answer.

Fatal Departure

"Hood Canal Reality, Lois Carter speaking, may I help you find a house?" she said.

"Ms. Carter, I talked with you about two months ago about the octagon house on the canal. My name is Steve Wilson."

"Oh yes, Mr. Wilson, I remember you. What can I do for you?"

"I'm really interested in the canal house. Is it still available?"

"No, it's temporarily off the market. Is there another house I can show you?"

"Sure, I would like to see another one, what do you have that's secluded?"

"I have just the one for you, can we meet?"

"Give me the address, I'll meet you there."

She opened her sales book and read the address from it. He thanked her and she said she would be there by two. He agreed and hung up.

He smiled and sat back in his car watching the woman through the window of her office. Now he would start his attack.

~~*~~

Dave came out of the store room smiling and adjusting his shirt. Sarah followed smiling. He went to the conference room and sat at the table, pulled his cell phone to call Seattle. Sarah went back to Mike's desk.

"Get a little in the back room," Chaz asked with a grin, petting Van Gogh as they sat by the desk.

"None of your business." She turned to Terry. "Looks like you will be going home. Dave is arranging for you be taken to your house. With police protection. We don't think Murdock will follow you, he's busy here, so if we get you out of town you will be safe."

"I hope so, but I haven't gotten my story yet."

"I'll be sure to get you the exclusive when they catch Murdock."

"Thanks, I've got the story of your ordeal just about finished. Would you like to read it?"

"Sure, just to be accurate."

Terry turned her laptop towards Sarah and she began to read.

About a half hour later, she finished. "This is very good, you touched on the high points and explained it very well. I approve." Sarah said with a smile.

"Thanks, Sarah. That's important to me."

Dave came out from the conference room and said, "Terry, get all your things together, I have a police officer coming from Olympia to pick you up and take you to your home. It's been good having you, but we need to get you out of the area, to give Murdock one less person to kill."

Terry laughed, "Actually, I appreciate that. I'd like to live to see my name on a byline of the paper. My things are in my car, I presume I will follow the officer?"

"That's the way it will be, you lead him though, he'll follow."

"Good, thank you so much for your hospitality. And saving my butt."

"Well, that was Chaz who did that, so thank him."

Terry looked to Chaz and thanked him. "If you are ever in Olympia, look me up." She smiled slyly.

Chaz blushed and said he would. Sarah grinned and then Dave left them all alone, laughing as he went.

*

Chapter 28

Everyone watched Terry drive out from the station in her red Corvette, followed by the Olympia Police patrol car. Dave felt relief now, with one less possible victim. They all went back in the station. Warren turned to the van before going in and smiled that Walt was still in the back playing with the equipment.

Virgil called to Dave, saying there was a call for him from Lois Carter. Dave went to his desk as Sarah came up behind him, curious as to what Lois would be calling about.

"Hello Lois, what's up?"

"Dave, I'm saying this under duress." Dave heard a slapping sound, then heard Lois yell, "You bastard, stop that."

He heard a voice say, "Go by the script, or I'll shove it down your fat throat."

Dave put his hand over the phone and told Virgil to try and trace the call. He listened again as Lois read from the paper Murdock had put in front of her. He told her to read it exactly as written and quickly. Dave figured he knew the time frame for tracing a call.

"Dave, you are requested to meet with Frank Murdock so he will be able to murder you and Sarah. If you don't come alone, no feds, he will murder..." she choked, ' He will murder me. So please come."

"Where to Lois?"

Dave heard the call hang up. He stared at the phone, amazed that he didn't get any information as to where to find them.

"Shit, Murdock has Lois."

Sarah went pale, "No, she can't be with him. No!"

201

Fatal Departure

Dave asked Virgil if he got anything. Virgil said he barely got hold of the phone company.

"Well, all we can do is wait. If Murdock wants us he'll call back. He won't hurt Lois, he needs her to get to us. She'll be safe for now."

"She better be, or I'll put my foot up Murdock's ass." Sarah said loudly.

Warren said he'd have Walt do a check on the phone call to see if they could get a number, he went out to get Walt.

Dave stood watching Sarah. She was tearing up and he didn't know what to say. He went to her and put his arms around her.

"Lois introduced us," Sarah said in a whisper. "She shouldn't have to go through this, not her. Dave, find her please."

"I'll do my best, but we need to find out where Murdock is."

Chaz spoke, "Maybe someone in Lois' office might know where she went to, start from there?"

Dave let Sarah go and said, "That's something. Lois has a secretary, she may know what Lois was up to." He went to the phone and after checking his phone book, he dialed.

"Hood Canal Realty. May I help you?" he heard in the receiver.

202

"Nora, this is Dave Chandler, can I ask you a question?"

"Sure, Sheriff. What's up?"

"Do you know where Lois is off to?" he said not wanting to upset the girl.

"She had an appointment to show a house for some man. Do you need her?"

"It's very important that I find her, can you give me the address of the house she went to and who was she going to meet?"

"Sure, hold on." The girl put the phone down and then came back with the address and a name. She gave it to Dave and he thanked her.

Warren and Walt were coming back in, as Dave went around the counter followed by Sarah and Chaz. Sarah had asked Virgil to watch Van Gogh after she tied him to the radiator.

"Follow me guys, I have an address to where Lois was going to meet with a man, according to Lois' secretary. It may be a long shot, but it's a start." They were just at the door when the desk phone rang, they stopped as Virgil answered.

He called to Dave, "It's for you. Lois."

Dave ran back to the phone and clicked on the recorder that tapes phone calls. "Lois, are you all right?"

Fatal Departure

"She's fine, for now, asshole. I'm going to play with you, make you suffer. Like you did to me."

"What did I do to you, I don't even know you!" Dave yelled into the phone.

"No, you don't know me, but that's not the point. When I have you in my power, I'll tell you the whole sordid story. Now wouldn't you like to know where I am?"

"It would help to catch you."

Dave heard him laugh. "Well said, but you won't catch me. I'll catch you and your little girlfriend. Now shut up and listen. You and your whore will go to your cute little house by the water, yes I knew about it, and wait for me. If I see one fed or any other cop anywhere nearby, I'll cut up your precious Lois in tiny pieces and dump them along your driveway. Don't fuck with me, I mean business. Tonight at seven. It will still be light enough for me to watch you drive in, without anyone else. Stay away until then, do what I say and maybe I'll let Lois go, maybe not. Your call." He hung up.

Dave stood for a moment then rewound the recording and played it for everyone. He shut it off after they all heard it.

"You're not going home without protection?" Warren asked.

"You heard what he said, I'm not playing with Lois' life."

"What about Sarah's life?" Chaz asked. "I want to be there to kick this guy's ass."

"Thanks Chaz, but let's play it according to his rules for now."

Walt said, "I can wire both of you and we can listen from down the road. There's no way he can watch everywhere."

Warren spoke. "I like that idea, and no argument Dave."

Dave looked to Sarah and nodded to Warren. "If you think it's going bad, come in fast. But not unless I say a certain word. That word will be pickles."

"Pickles? What kind of an emergency word it that?"

"Something no one would say in a crime scene. Now get us wired."

Walt led then out to the van and pulled out a box full of wired equipment all neatly wrapped and labeled. He pulled two sets of wires and proceeded to attach the devices to Dave and Sarah. He tested the receiver to be sure it was picking up their signals. He gave them thumbs up and they stood out by the cars.

"Now what?" Warren asked.

Dave looked at this watch and said, "We have three hours before we go. We can still go to the house that Lois was supposed to meet Murdock. Maybe we can get a trail from there."

Fatal Departure

"Works for me," Warren said.

Dave turned to Sarah and Chaz, "You two stay here, it's better to separate the two of us. He wants us together so stay away from me for now. We can check the house, but I doubt there will be anything there."

"What about our house? He said we were to stay away until seven. Maybe he's hiding out there until then?"

"That's true, but if he sees us near there, Lois will be in danger. So we wait." He turned to Warren and said to go. They went out the front and to the cars. Walt said he was driving the van. "You signed for it, it's in your care," Warren told him with a grin.

They drove away as Sarah and Chaz watched from the porch. She turned to Chaz, "So are we going to the house? I need to see if I left the stove on."

Chaz smiled and said, "You're going to piss Dave off, but I was told to follow you anywhere you go."

"Then follow me," she said and walked to her car. "I remember that Harcourt was able to watch the house from the woods next door, and he hid his car down the road." I think we can retrace his steps and see if Murdock is at the house."

"Couldn't you have told Dave that?"

"He would have said the same thing, Murdock said don't go near the house."

"Not that you listen." Chaz smiled as they pulled out of the station parking.

Virgil came to the door and looked out to see everyone was gone. He went back to his desk and said to Van Gogh, "I guess we're in charge now."

Dave led the men to a house out in the sticks of the town. It was a secluded house that hadn't sold for over a year. It was run down and priced too high. Dave thought that Lois liked to try and sell shacks for a good price.

They stopped down the road from the house and walked up. Walt stayed in the van listening to the wire Dave wore. He said he'd come running if they needed him. As they approached the house, they could see Lois' car, Dave recognized it.

"Well we have the right house. You go that way, I'll attack this way and don't shoot me please." Dave grinned, as they split up.

Dave ran up to the house and stopped by a window, looking in carefully. He saw no one in what would be the living room. He went to another window and looked in, then went to the back door and tried the knob, it turned. He slowly went in listening for any noise. He heard none so far. Then he heard someone walking towards him from the other room, he raised his gun ready to fire. A man came around the corner of the kitchen with a gun, Dave took aim and froze. It was Warren.

*

Chapter 29

Sarah and Chaz crept up from the south of the house, hidden by the trees and brush. They peeked through the bushes towards the house, but saw no vehicles around the building. Sarah remembered back when she was running through these bushes trying to get away from Max Draegon, the NY Slasher. It gave her a chill.

"Maybe he's not here yet," Sarah said to Chaz.

"Maybe we should get out of here," Chaz replied.

"Not until I'm certain he's not here. You big wuss."

"And what good is that going to do? He'll be here eventually, and I'd like to have you away from here. And I'm not a wuss."

"Well then, let's go check the house. Besides, I need something."

"What?"

"Something feminine, you don't want to know."

Chaz shut up and followed her to the house. She came up the rear and to the back door. She pulled her keys and unlocked the door. She listened and then went in. Chaz had his Magnum out ready to fire at anything that moved.

They went through the house, he wasn't there. No sign that anyone had been in the house, since they left this morning. "He's not here, maybe we should go back."

"Good idea, listen to yourself. We need to be back before Dave returns and finds out you left the station." They went back out the door and over to their car.

On the other side of town, Dave and Warren were examining the house were Lois was taken from. "Good place to grab her, secluded, no one around and easy to put her in a car and drive away."

Warren picked up a used roll of duct tape carefully, and called Walt through Dave's microphone. "Walt come on in, I have some evidence you may want."

"Well, we know he was here, so was Lois. They'd have to be in the canal house or on the road hiding until later." Dave said.

"So all we can do now is wait, then play it by ear." Warren said and watched for Walt to drive in. They went outside, as Dave called the station.

"Virgil, put Sarah on," He asked.

"Uh, well… she's not here."

"Okay, where is she?"

"I don't know, she and Chaz drove off after you left. '

209

Fatal Departure

Dave thanked him and hung up. "Crap, you tell a woman not to do something and she does it. I hope Chaz is alert, not just for the killer, but for Sarah."

Warren laughed and took the tape to Walt, now getting out of the van. He opened an envelope and put it in. He closed it and took it back to the van.

"I suppose he has a crime lab in the back?" Dave said laughing.

"Actually, he does. He'll have the prints off the roll and sent into IAFIS and CODIS for a match before we get back to the station. It's a good bet they belong to Murdock." Warren spoke as they went to the patrol car.

"Aren't you going back with Walt?"

"No, he can have his fun for now. I don't want to wait for him to come up with his match."

Warren waved to Walt and they drove off.

Sarah and Chaz got back to the station before Dave, she figured she was safe. They went in and Virgil said, "Dave called for you about twenty minutes ago, I said I didn't know where you went."

"Okay, that's good. We need to work on an alibi." Sarah said to Chaz.

"Why would you need an alibi?" Came a voice from behind her. It was Dave just coming in.

"Hi honey, what did you find at the house?"

"I should ask what did you find at our house?"

She smiled then said quietly, "Nothing, no one there. We were careful though."

Dave looked to Chaz, "You're fired."

"Hey, don't blame him, he did exactly what you told him, to follow me around. You didn't say he couldn't keep me from getting in trouble. Now re-hire him."

"Okay, Chaz, you're re-hired. But from now on you stop her from getting into trouble."

"It would be my pleasure," Chaz laughed.

Dave smiled, "We found Lois' car but no Lois. They were there, but long gone. If he wasn't in the canal house, as you found out, he's probably driving around. It would be nice knowing what kind of car he has."

"We don't, so we just wait."

~~*~~

Murdock was not happy that Sarah had broken his orders. He saw her going into the house with the biker. He wanted Dave and her together, so he waited. He could hear Lois in the trunk moving around, but she would be fine for now. He waited until he saw them leave and drove in the drive. He pulled the car around the back of the house on the lawn and parked.

Fatal Departure

He opened up the trunk and pulled Lois up and out. She was making noise but the duct tape over her mouth prevented her from talking. Murdock went to the back door, it was locked and he didn't want to bother with picking the lock. He pulled his revolver and shot out the glass of the door.

Lois hoped the alarms were on for the breaking of the glass. It was what tripped up the Slasher back when he broke out a window. Maybe they would know in the station that he was in the house. Murdock pushed her through the door and went to get a chair from the dining table and put it in the middle of the living room. He pushed her into the chair and tied her to it. Then he went to the kitchen and checked to see what was in the refrigerator. He found the beer that they had and took a can. He didn't want to be drunk, but one can would take the edge off him.

He still had an hour and a half, so he went to the TV and turned it on. He sat on the couch and enjoyed some movie. He had to move over to see around Lois.

~~*~~

The men stood looking at the map on the wall, Dave was pointing out places for Warren to sit and wait for his signal as needed. He showed Virgil and Mike, who came in for this, where to wait for any help they may need.

"Just keep low so Murdock doesn't see you. No sense in getting Lois killed. Or us," Dave added. "Well we have a half hour, let's go get in place."

They all left and went to their cars. Dave noticed that Walt wasn't back yet. "Warren, where's Walt?"

"He's still running tests on the tape, it takes time. I do wish he were here though."

"Okay, you can go with Mike in his car. Hey, if Walt has the van, how are you going to hear us?"

"Uh, I didn't think of that. I'll call him." He was pulling out his cell phone, just as Walt drove up. He got out and came over to the men.

"Did you get a match?"

"It's still running, I knew it was getting close to time, so came in."

"Good. I wanted to hear what they are saying. Is the recording equipment ready to go?"

"Yep, it's all set."

Dave said, ' Okay, let's roll." Dave took Sarah in his Bronco, letting Virgil and Mike use the patrol cars. Walt and Warren were behind in the van as they drove down the 101 Highway towards the house. Dave pulled over to the place they agreed on to wait. It was secluded and off the road, so they wouldn't be seen easily. Dave looked at his watch, they had ten minutes to final attack.

Dave took Sarah and gave her a Kevlar vest and had her put a jacket over the protective covering. She didn't like the weight of the thing but it hopefully would help keep her alive. "If there's shooting, dive for the nearest cover," he told her.

They got into the car and Dave said into his mic, "Hello, can you hear me now." He could see Warren laughing in the van and he waved. "Okay, curtain time."

They drove out and down the road finally coming up to the drive of the house. Dave was nervous, as he pulled in, slowly. He was watching the house, no sign of movement, but that didn't mean they weren't being watched. He did notice the front door was wide open.

He parked at the porch and they got out. He heard a voice from the vestibule. "Come on in, said the spider to the flies."

Sarah said quietly next to Dave, "More like a cockroach."

They went to the door, and slowly went in, with Dave leading Sarah. "I certainly hope you didn't bring your gun." Came a voice from the living room.

"I'm unarmed. Can't say the same for you."

"Right, I am armed and the gun is pointing at your mouthy friend."

They came around the corner of the wall leading into the living room and saw Lois tied to a chair in the middle of the room, Murdock was standing behind her with a gun pointed at her head.

Dave didn't recognize the man from anywhere, having only seen the photo of him.

"Come in my friends, welcome to your nightmare."

"Screw you Murdock, why are you doing this?"

"Oh, don't be so crude. Sit down and I'll tell you my story.

~~*~~

In the van down the road, the computer made a dinging noise. Walt went to the screen and read what was on it. "I got a match to the prints, but you're not going to believe it." Walt said.

"Is it Murdock?"

"Well, yes and no. Murdock is an alias, one of a few. You're not going to believe what is his real name."

*

Chapter 30

"So, are you going to explain how we made you mad enough to want to kill us?"

"You just don't get it," he said coming around Lois and straddling another chair he had out. "I've dropped clues every time I've talked to you."

Fatal Departure

"Okay, I'm not wanting to figure out anything right now. Just talk."

"Tsk, tsk, Dave. You are supposed to be an officer of the law and be able to solve crimes. Or do you just shoot people?"

"I've only shot and killed one person in my career as a cop..." He paused as a thought came to him. "That person I shot was Max Draegon, the NY Slasher, and he deserved to die."

"Max Draegon, yes, he was a mean, vicious man. But he taught me how to kill and to be as ruthless as he was. And you killed him, my father. Allow me to introduce myself, Frank Draegon."

Sarah felt a chill being in front of the son of the man who almost killed her. "Your father tried to kill me, and he killed Derek Harcourt in this room. Not to mention all the innocent women off the streets. He was a monster, a bastard and he deserved to die."

Murdock, AKA Frank Draegon, came up from his chair pointing his gun at her. "Shut up, he was my father and you have no right to berate him."

Sarah turned her head to Dave's shoulder avoiding Draegon's gaze. He waited and then sat back down. "I'm not going to kill you yet, I want to make you suffer. Maybe I'll shoot little parts of you slowly. I'll start with Sarah, just so you can watch her suffer. I'll start with her feet, so she can't run, like she did from my father. Then, when I run out of her parts, I'll start with you Dave."

Dave was holding his temper, he was at a disadvantage, Draegon had the gun. Now he wished the Calvary would rush in.

"Well, this is a pickle isn't it?" Dave said loudly.

Sarah looked to him and wondered what he was up to. Draegon stood looking to the window. "Are you up to something Dave?" He went to the window looking out. It was still light enough to see around the area, he saw nothing. "I hope you aren't giving any signals to anyone, that wouldn't be nice."

He came back to Lois, pointing the gun at her head. "Now what shall I do with this one? She's a liability. She knows me and I can't have any witnesses."

"What does that matter, there are feds who know who you are. They'll find you even if you kill us. My friends won't rest until they get you."

"I'll be long gone, I have a small motorboat on the canal tied up behind the house. After I kill you, I'm out of here." He grinned like he had the upper hand. "I have a larger boat out in the canal waiting, it's a big boat, big enough to take me around the coast to LA, where I'll start my career back up following in my father's footsteps. Too bad Sarah, you won't be able to finish your book, my father wasn't happy with Harcourt's book. I'd probably hate yours."

He came around to them and pointed his gun at Sarah's feet, she cringed.

217

Fatal Departure

The front door suddenly crashed open and Warren came flying in with his gun pointed at Draegon. The man turned, as Warren pulled the trigger, just missing Draegon. He turned towards the back door but saw Chaz standing outside with a big silver gun aimed at him. He turned again as everyone was firing. He made it to the hallway towards the side door and burst out, finding Walt with his gun aimed at him. He brought his gun up and fired, hitting Walt, he went down.

Draegon ran in the direction of the boat, jumping the rail on the cliff edge down to the shoreline. He got to the boat but it wasn't there. He looked out and saw the boat floating away.

"Missing something?" He heard the voice above him and turned to see Chaz with a bead on him. Draegon took a chance and ran down the shoreline as Chaz was firing. Draegon got to another short cliff and climbed up. He came face to face with Dave. Draegon raised his gun as Warren fired at him from the side. Draegon got a shocked look on his face, then he went down.

"Damn, I so wanted to do that. Now I can say I got the son of the NY Slasher." Warren was smiling widely. Chaz came running up and they all stood looking at the lifeless body of Draegon. Virgil and Mike came up and Dave told them to watch the body until the M.E. could get there.

"Where's Walt?" Warren asked. No One knew. He ran off and around the building followed by Dave and Chaz.

Bob Moats

He came around the side of the house and found Walt on the ground. "Shit, no!" he yelled as he went to Walt. He checked his pulse, and yelled to Dave to call for an EMS. Dave called the local hospital and asked for assistance.

"Come on Walt, hang in there. I need you, man. I can't operate all that crap in the van without you." He was checking the wound, it wasn't bleeding badly, but there could be internal damage.

About twenty minutes later, the paramedics had Walt on a gurney and put him in the ambulance. Dave and Sarah had gone back in the living room to release Lois, who was fuming now. "Sorry Lois, we got him, I know you wanted a piece of him, sorry."

"That's alright, I have a great story to tell all my friends now." She was happy as Dave told Mike to drive her to her car. They left as Virgil said, "The M.E. has the body all wrapped up. Do you want me to call forensics?"

"I don't think so, there's no mystery now. Just a lot of paperwork. I'll let Warren handle most of it."

"Where is Warren?" Sarah asked

"He followed the EMS to the hospital. He wanted to be with Walt."

"I hope he's all right?"

"One of the paramedics said it didn't look like the bullet hit anything vital. He'll live, but I don't know if Warren will. He's a wreck."

219

Fatal Departure

Dave looked around the living room and to the door that Draegon blasted. "I hope the alarm worked, but there was no one in the station to hear it."

"Oh, oh. Van Gogh is still there. I hope the alarm is not buzzing continuously. Poor puppy, he'll be shell shocked."

"Virgil, go rescue Van Gogh and bring him back here. I don't really want to go into the station tonight to fill out paperwork. We'll get to it in the morning."

Virgil went off and Sarah went to the kitchen and took two beers out of the refrigerator. She came back and handed one to Dave. "Ah, the golden brew. Much needed after the day we had. I think we need a vacation now, some where far from here."

"How about New York, we could visit my friends and I could show you off."

"That's a possibility, I'll think on it."

Later in the evening, Dave sat with Sarah, relaxing on the couch. Chaz was in an easy chair drinking his beer and watching TV.

Warren had called earlier and said that Walt was going to be alright, they'd patch him up and release him in the morning. Warren even braved calling the Director and told him about the whole incident. "Walt and I are up for commendations," he said proudly. He added that he'd be back at the house shortly.

"Well, we can get back to our own bed now." Dave whispered in Sarah's ear.

"I heard that," Chaz said, but not looking at them.

Dave threw a pillow from the couch at Chaz. "You know you are out of work now. We got the killer."

"Yep, but I might just hang around for a while, do some fishing on the canal. Or I may go to Olympia and visit Terry, she did say to look her up."

"Fishing or Terry, what a dilemma. Do you have a fishing license?" Dave asked him.

"Damn, I forgot to get one, guess it will be Olympia, then."

Sarah laughed, stood and came over to Chaz. She kissed him on his bald head and said, "Give her your best."

He smiled and said, "I intend to."

~~*~~

The next week came and all was quiet once again in the town. The citizens were all happy that the killer was caught and life went on as if nothing happened. Of course, Lois was a local celebrity, she was spreading the word about her ordeal.

"She was tied up the whole time and she's the hero?" Sarah said as she sat at Mike's desk with Van Gogh next to her.

Fatal Departure

"Don't fault the woman, let her have her moment. Besides, everyone knows the real story, so she's not fooling anyone." Dave spoke from the bulletin board where he was putting up new wanted posters.

"Do you have to put those up?" Sarah asked.

"Yep, if one of these men come into town, I want to know what they look like."

"God, I don't want to see another criminal around here ever again." She laughed.

The front door opened and in came Warren and Walt, both looking refreshed. "Hey crime fighters," Warren said as he shook Dave's hand.

"What are you doing here?" Dave asked.

"The Director of the Seattle office of the FBI wanted me to give this to you. Walt handed Warren a large envelope and he opened it. He took out a sheet of paper, it was a certificate.

"Dave, the Seattle FBI and the Seattle Police both wanted to give this to you for helping to catch Draegon. It's a commendation for heroic bravery in the face of death."

"Stop being so dramatic," Dave laughed and took the certificate. He pinned it to the bulletin board next to the wanted posters.

"We did some digging at Frank Draegon's home and found enough evidence that connected Draegon to the killing of the Seattle detective. Case closed."

"Good, I hope there are no other relatives of Max Draegon to come after us."

"Nope we got them all. Say Sarah, how's your nightmares doing?"

"Haven't had a one since this ordeal ended. I talked to Dr. Gladwin the other day and we got a few things settled. I'm hopefully cured now."

"Great. So, we just came to give you this, and now we have to go to Olympia. There's a threat of a terrorist cell possibly in the area."

"Crap, don't chase them up here. I don't think the town can take it."

"We won't, so what are your plans now?"

"Sarah and I are taking a week or two off and going to New York to visit her friends."

Warren laughed and said, "I'll call ahead and warn the New York FBI to expect you."

Dave laughed. "You do that my friend, you do that."

THE END

Fatal Departure

Bonus Preview of the third book of the Fatal Series "Fatal Romance"

Chapter 1

The plain looking woman entered the bar and sat at the table where she had been instructed to sit. She smiled as the waitress came up and asked what she wanted. She didn't want to drink before she met with her date, so she ordered a soda. The waitress went off and the woman looked around the dingy looking bar. She thought it was a strange place to meet with the man she hadn't met before. She had received a reply to her personal dating ad in the New York Times, from a man saying he would like to meet with her for a social drink. They exchanged information by email, no phone calls, and he suggested they meet here. It was an old bar, probably built in the late twenties. It had ceiling fans and old light fixtures that were most likely shiny and bright at one time.

Her drink came and she dipped into her purse and gave the girl a five. The girl gave her the change, two dollars. The woman thought three dollars was a bit pricey for soda, but she didn't intend to buy another. She glanced at her watch, he was ten minutes late. Maybe he wouldn't even show. Another useless night, she thought, hoping for a man to romance her, wine and dine her. Maybe they'd go back to her apartment for late night love making. She blushed at the thought.

Thirty minutes later, she was starting to feel foolish, waiting for a man who wasn't coming. She started to stand to leave when the door opened and in walked a man. He stopped just inside the door as the woman sat back down. He came to her and said, "I really apologize for my lateness, work and traffic, I hope you understand?"

She looked up to the man; he had deep brown eyes and a handsome face. Her heart skipped a few beats and she said, "No problem. I am a patient person, and I understand how life can get in the way."

"Very good, I like you already," he said with a smile that gave her pause and a catch in her throat. She had hopes for a good night. Unfortunately, it would be her last night on earth.

~~*~~

Sarah was having a fit trying to get through the Homeland Security checks at the Sea-Tac International Airport just below Seattle, Washington. She wasn't happy with the intrusion into her life and all the examinations they were doing to her baggage. Dave Chandler, her live-in love and Sheriff of Jefferson County, where they shared a house together, was trying not to laugh.

"If I hear one giggle from you, I'm cutting you off the rest of our vacation," she threatened. "I don't like my underwear being searched for explosives."

Dave had to show his ID to the guard and she noticed his badge. "Are you a law officer?" the TSA agent asked.

"Yes ma'am, Sheriff of Jefferson County," he replied

"Well Sheriff, you can go right on to the boarding gate."

Fatal Departure

Sarah looked at the woman and said tersely, "I'm with him, can I go on?"

Dave leaned to the woman and said quietly, "She's my prisoner, I need to have her close."

The TSA agent smiled and said, "Then you should handcuff her." She chuckled and let them both through.

Sarah at least waited until she was out of earshot of the woman and said, "I heard that prisoner crack, I'll let it go this time, but you are on thin ice."

"Can we just get in the plane before you start an international incident?"

"I'll be good, until we get in the air."

"That doesn't work either; they can land the plane at the next airport and boot you off. I'm not going on to Vegas and then New York without you."

"Okay, but I'm writing a letter of objection to someone. This is a poor way to run an airline."

"It's not the airline, it's the government, and you can't fight with them."

"I want to fight with someone. So find out who I can complain to."

"I'll do that dear, now take a breath and let's get through this in one piece."

They went to the boarding gate and showed their boarding passes to the man at the door. He smiled and welcomed them aboard. Sarah held her tongue as they passed through the door and down the corridor to the plane. The passageway in the plane was narrow and crowded, people trying to get their carry-on luggage in the overhead compartments. Dave found their seats, Sarah insisted on a window seat and it was arranged. She slid into the seat and looked out at the tarmac of the terminal where the plane was resting.

"Not a very pretty sight," she said to Dave.

"Wait until we're in the air, I'm sure it gets better. It's going to be a short flight anyway. Our first stop will be Las Vegas, where we will spend a couple days relaxing and losing our money. Then we catch another flight to New York, by way of Minneapolis, Detroit then into JFK. A day and a half of layovers and stale pretzels in plastic bags that are impossible to open. Oh joy."

"Well, you made the arrangements for this trip, blame yourself. I had enough money to fly us first class all the way, but no, you wanted to save a few dollars." She turned to the window as the plane was ready to leave the airport terminal.

Dave smiled and sat back, he had never been on a plane before so this would be interesting. The plane began to taxi out to the runway and then must have gotten permission from the tower to take-off. Dave held on to the arms of the seat, until his knuckles were white. Sarah put her hand on his and said, "Hold on dear, it won't be a long flight." She patted his hand and watched out the window

Fatal Departure

as the plane took off. For the next one hour and forty-five minutes, they sat enjoying the trip.

The plane descended into McCarran International Airport in Las Vegas and landed without so much as a bump. Everyone departed from the plane and went to get their baggage. Dave found their bags and they went out to the taxi stands. They managed to get a taxi and told the man to take them to the Bellagio Hotel where Dave had made reservations. The taxi dropped them off at the entrance and they took their bags, went into the hotel and up to the desk.

"Yes, Mr. Chandler, we have your room ready. Here's a packet of fun things to do while in Vegas." The girl at the desk signed them in and called for a porter to take them to their room.

The elevator ride was fast and they came out on the tenth floor, as the porter led them to their room for the next two days. Dave tipped the porter and he went off. Sarah was standing in the middle of the huge room looking at all the luxurious surroundings. She turned to Dave and said, "I love it."

Dave went off to the side where the bedroom was and said, "Guess what I found?"

Sarah was looking out the window at the strip of casinos and hotels and said, "What?"

"A very large bed, shall we kick off our vacation to a good start."

Bob Moats

Sarah turned and ran to him. He picked her up and carried her into the bedroom.

~~*~~

The man was studying the New York Times newspaper classifieds for any personal lonely hearts posting. He read down the list of ads and wrote down a few of them on a pad he carried. He studied the names and picked one he thought would be a good choice. Lonely, plain, hard up and willing, the kind he liked.

He sat at his desk and opened the laptop to reply to the first one he decided on. A woman named Lisa, in the Bronx. He typed out the reply to her ad and then when he was satisfied, he sent it. Now it was time to get rid of the last body he had, the woman from the bar.

He stood , went to his garage and opened the trunk of his car, looking to the body laid out all nice and silent. The way he liked his women. He closed the trunk, opened the garage door and drove out. It was just getting dark as he went up the South Belt Parkway to Spring Creek Park, just off Jamaica Bay. It was marshy and secluded where he turned off and pulled his car to a stop. He got out and was looking around the area for anyone else wandering the park. He saw no one; it was a bit chilly for anyone to be near the water. He went over to the area he had used many times before. It was damp and full of reeds, covering the bodies he had dumped there before.

He went back to his car and looked around again. No one was watching, so he opened the trunk and took the woman out, carrying her to his dump spot. He placed her in the reeds and spread her out so she could decompose quickly. Her naked body lay on the wet ground as he pulled brush from the ground and covered her with them. He heard the roar of the jets from JFK Airport, just north of where he stood. He watched the massive planes leaving and arriving at the huge airport, going and coming from places around the globe.

He didn't care, he liked his own little space he created, his little grave yard of women he used and threw away. He smiled and went back to his car, back to his home to check his e-mail for the next victim.

*

Continued in the book.

Bob Moats

The Jim Richards series of books by Bob Moats

For a preview or to purchase a book, go to
http://murdernovels.com